EXSPELLED

MORGANA BEST

GLOSSARY

Some Australian spellings and expressions are entirely different from US spellings and expressions. Below are just a few examples.

It would take an entire book to list all the differences.

For example, people often think "How are you going?" (instead of "How are you doing?") is an error, but it's normal and correct for Aussies!

The author has used Australian spelling in this series. Here are a few examples: *Mum* instead of the US spelling *Mom*, *neighbour* instead of the US spelling *neighbor*, *realise* instead of the US spelling *realize*. It is *Ms*, *Mr* and *Mrs* in Australia, not *Ms.*, *Mr.* and *Mrs.*; *defence* not *defense; judgement* not *judgment; cosy* and not *cozy; 1930s* not *1930's; offence* not *offense; centre* not *center; towards* not *toward; jewellery* not *jewelry; favour* not *favor; mould* not *mold; two storey house* not *two story house; practise* (verb) not *practice* (verb); *odour* not *odor; smelt* not *smelled; travelling* not *traveling; liquorice* not *licorice; cheque* not *check; leant* not *leaned; have concussion* not *have a concussion; anti clockwise* not *counterclockwise; go to hospital* not *go to the hospital; sceptic* not *skeptic; aluminium* not *aluminum; learnt* not *learned.* We have *fancy dress* parties not *costume* parties. We don't say *gotten.* We say *car crash* (or *accident*) not *car wreck.* We say *a herb* not *an herb* as we pronounce the 'h.'

The above are just a few examples.

It's not just different words; Aussies sometimes use different expressions in sentence structure. We might *eat a curry* not *eat curry.* We might say *in the main street* not *on the main street.* Someone might be *going well* instead of *doing well.* We might say *without drawing breath* not *without drawing a breath.*

These are just some of the differences.

Please note that these are not mistakes or typos, but correct, normal Aussie spelling, terms, and syntax.

AUSTRALIAN SLANG AND TERMS

Benchtops - counter tops (kitchen)

Big Smoke - a city

Blighter - infuriating or good-for-nothing person

Blimey! - an expression of surprise

Bloke - a man (usually used in nice sense, "a good bloke")

Blue (noun) - an argument ("to have a blue")

Bluestone - copper sulphate (copper sulfate in US spelling)

Bluo - a blue laundry additive, an optical brightener

Boot (car) - trunk (car)

Bonnet (car) - hood (car)

Bore - a drilled water well

Budgie smugglers (variant: budgy smugglers) - named after the Aussie native bird, the budgerigar. A slang term for brief and tight-fitting men's swimwear

Bugger! - as an expression of surprise, not a swear word

Bugger - as in "the poor bugger" - refers to an unfortunate person (not a swear word)

Bunging it on - faking something, pretending

Bush telegraph - the grapevine, the way news spreads by word of mouth in the country

Car park - parking lot

Cark it - die

Chooks - chickens

Come good - turn out okay

Copper, cop - police officer

Coot - silly or annoying person

Cream bun - a sweet bread roll with copious amounts of cream, plus jam (= jelly in US) in the centre

Crook - 1. "Go crook (on someone)" - to berate them. 2. (someone is) crook - (someone is) ill. 3. Crook (noun) - a criminal

Demister (in car) - defroster

Drongo - an idiot

Dunny - an outhouse, a toilet, often ramshackle

Fair crack of the whip - a request to be fair, reasonable, just

Flannelette (fabric) - cotton, wool, or synthetic fabric, one side of which has a soft finish.

Flat out like a lizard drinking water - very busy

Galah - an idiot

Garbage - trash

G'day - Hello

Give a lift (to someone) - give a ride (to someone)

Goosebumps - goose pimples

Gumboots - rubber boots, wellingtons

Knickers - women's underwear

Laundry (referring to the room) - laundry room

Lamingtons - iconic Aussie cakes, square, sponge, chocolate-dipped, and coated with desiccated coconut. Some have a layer of cream and strawberry jam (= jelly in US) between the two halves.

Lift - elevator

Like a stunned mullet - very surprised

Mad as a cut snake - either insane or very angry

Mallee bull (as fit as, as mad as) - angry and/or fit, robust, super strong.

Miles - while Australians have kilometres these days, it is common to use expressions such as, "The road stretched for miles," "It was miles away."

Moleskins - woven heavy cotton fabric with suede-like finish, commonly used as working wear, or as town clothes

Mow (grass / lawn) - cut (grass / lawn)

Neenish tarts - Aussie tart. Pastry base. Filling is based on sweetened condensed milk mixture or mock cream. Some have layer of raspberry jam (jam = jelly in US). Topping is in two equal halves: icing (= frosting in US), usually chocolate on one side, and either lemon or pink on the other.

Pub - The pub at the south of a small town is often referred to as the 'bottom pub' and the pub at the north end of town, the 'top pub.' The size of a small town is often judged by the number of pubs - i.e. "It's a three pub town."

Red cattle dog - (variant: blue cattle dog usually known as a 'blue dog') - referring to the breed of Australian Cattle Dog. However, a 'red dog' is usually a red kelpie (another breed of dog)

Shoot through - leave

Shout (a drink) - to buy a drink for someone

Skull (a drink) - drink a whole drink without stopping

Stone the crows! - an expression of surprise

Takeaway (food) - Take Out (food)

Toilet - also refers to the room if it is separate from the bathroom

Torch - flashlight

Tuck in (to food) - to eat food hungrily

Ute / Utility - pickup truck

Vegemite - Australian food spread, thick, dark brown

Wardrobe - closet

Windscreen - windshield

Indigenous References

Bush tucker - food that occurs in the Australian bush

Koori - the original inhabitants/traditional custodians of the land of Australia in the part of NSW in which this book is set. *Murri* are the people just to the north. White European culture often uses the term, *Aboriginal people*.

CHAPTER 1

J shook the rain from my umbrella and left it in an ancient porcelain umbrella stand just inside the front door of Ruprecht's store, *Glinda's.* Unfortunately, I wasn't able to shake the rain from my clothes. It was a miserable wet day in Bayberry Creek, and I was drenched from head to toe. Anyone would have thought it was winter and not summer. Even *Glinda's* had taken on an uncustomary dismal atmosphere.

"It's wild out there tonight," my best friend and employee, Thyme, said by way of greeting.

I nodded, wiped the rain from my eyes, and followed her through the maze of antique furniture to Ruprecht's apartment directly behind his store.

I could tell something was going on as soon I walked into the kitchen and saw Ruprecht, his granddaughter, Mint, and Camino sitting around the large wooden table. "This is an intervention," Camino announced happily.

I must have looked shocked, because Ruprecht hurried to correct her. "No, of course it's not, Amelia!" His eyebrows shot skyward. "It's a surprise." He pushed a golden envelope across the table to me and gestured to me to sit down.

I did so and picked up the envelope. "A golden ticket! Am I going to Willie Wonka's chocolate factory?" I had an insane desire to giggle. It must have been the stress of the last week.

Ruprecht smiled. "Open it."

I opened the envelope, and there indeed was a ticket, but it wasn't to a chocolate factory—it had the words, *Paradise Island Cooking School* emblazoned in bold black writing across the top of a photograph of a tropical island.

"After everything you've been through with that man trying to murder you the other day, we all got together and decided to send you away to a remote island," Camino said excitedly.

I frowned. Mercifully, Ruprecht interrupted

her. "It's not a punishment or anything like that, quite the contrary. You've been working long hours, a man just tried to kill you, and you've had to contend with your house. I mean, how many other people can say they have a living house?"

"Not many," I answered truthfully. "The house is like a weird housemate, but at least it protects me."

Everyone nodded and Thyme patted my arm. "Now, you know how your cooking's been improving, and we've explained to you that it's because you're just starting to use your powers as a witch?" It was my turn to nod. Thyme pressed on. "We all thought you should get away and have a nice vacation, so we're sending you to a lovely cooking school on a tropical island, all expenses paid."

Nice vacation. Cooking school. Wasn't that a contradiction in terms? I tried to process the information. "So you're sending me to a cooking school on a tropical island?" I did my best to look excited as I said it.

Ruprecht beamed. "Yes! A whole week, with luxury accommodation on a beautiful tropical island in the Pacific Ocean. To be precise, it's in the Whitsundays, off the coast of Queensland. You'll have peace and quiet and solitude, for a whole week."

"And cooking lessons?" I asked.

Everybody smiled and nodded.

I bit my lip. "Their insurance premiums will go up."

Ruprecht handed me a cup of tea. I hadn't even seen him leave the table. "Amelia, you exaggerate. You haven't set a kitchen on fire with your baking, since, um, when?"

"Not for a month," Thyme responded cheerfully.

I did not share their confidence. I was the world's worst cook. I had set rooms on fire, sent people to the hospital with food poisoning, and my cupcakes had even cracked concrete on more than one occasion. However, my poor baking ability was strangely linked with my (not poor) abilities as a witch. The fact that I had recently started to embrace those abilities had encouraged everyone —everyone, that is, except me. I finally found my voice. "I can't shut the shop for a week," I protested feebly.

"Nonsense!" Thyme said. "Business is picking up, and it would make sound business sense if you could learn to produce cupcakes to keep up with the higher turnover. So just take a week off and relax, and learn to cook. Mint can replace you at the store."

And so it was decided. I was to be replaced by Mint and shipped off to a secluded island in the middle of nowhere—or in the Pacific Ocean just off the coast of Queensland, to be precise— an island which, knowing my luck, was probably populated by cannibals and surrounded by sharks.

I looked up to see Thyme eyeing me speculatively. "Unless, of course, you want to stay in town because you'll miss *someone*?"

I glared at her. Thyme had caught me kissing the magnificent Alder Vervain and hadn't let me hear the end of it since. If only she knew I had kissed him more thoroughly since, *sans* an audience. Tingles ran through me at the thought. My mind drifted off into a pleasant daydream about Alder, when Camino's voice snapped me back to reality.

"I bought you a onesie as a gift to take to the island," she said, delighted.

I grimaced, but managed to turn it into the semblance of a smile. "Wonderful! Is it the bandicoot one you mentioned last week? Or a tiger snake? Maybe a funnel-web spider?"

Camino laughed. "Oh Amelia, I'll miss your sense of humour when you've gone. No, it's a fruit bat."

"A bat?" I squeaked. "That's very kind of you. Bats carry the deadly Lyssavirus, don't they?"

Camino nodded happily. "Yes, and the Hendra virus too, which is completely incurable."

Mint waved a pamphlet at me in an obvious attempt to save the situation. "Amelia, you don't need to worry. It's a whole week of cooking lessons for beginners." She pointed to the pamphlet. "It's for people to learn how to cook using the domestic appliances that they'd have in their own home. There are classes on health and safety, and information on nutrition. The classes include all ingredients and recipes. You'll be given all the recipe notes to bring home." She smiled reassuringly as she handed me the pamphlet.

I read the concluding words: *Just bring yourself, roll up your sleeves, and have fun. The minimum age is eight years.*

Perhaps it *was* my level, after all. I regarded the photo of the island with renewed interest. It did look a tranquil setting with the turquoise sea and the brilliant white sand flanked by towering palm trees.

I took a deep breath and smiled. I might as well enjoy myself. "Thank you, I'll do it! What could possibly go wrong?"

CHAPTER 2

Of course, I should have known not to say, 'What could possibly go wrong?' The last time I uttered those words was during a thunderstorm. I said those words as I turned on the TV which was promptly struck by lightning and exploded. I still had the burn marks on my arm, years later.

Still, there was no chance I would be struck by lightning today. The sky was clear and the waters were calm. I was on my way to Paradise Island in a boat, thankfully a large boat, and the island was only a two hour boat journey from the mainland. It was all quite civilised, not to mention safe. The on-board coffee was even good, and I was making the acquaintance of some of my fellow students. All in all, it was turning out to be a pleasant experience.

"I've been there before," a woman announced proudly. She had previously introduced herself as Lisa Lewis. I wondered why a woman who had been to the cooking school before would need to return to take beginner cooking classes. Perhaps there were worse cooks in existence than I was, after all. That was encouraging. I studied the woman. I was never any good at guessing someone's age, but she looked to be in her late thirties. The abundance of her make-up was exceeded only by the all-too-fake blackness of her hair, which contrasted rather unpleasantly with the inch of pale colour along the roots. She was overly dressed for a boat ride, down to spiky high heels and a rather short skirt. I thought she would not look out of place standing on a street corner in a seedy area, but then I silently berated myself for my unkindness.

The tall, distinguished man sitting next to her spoke up. "I find this boat ride rather distasteful." His accent was British and rather posh. He reminded me strongly of Benedict Cumberbatch, only older. He extended a hand to me. "Hello, I'm Benedict…"—he paused as I gasped—"Fletcher. What do you do?"

"What do I do?" I repeated stupidly. I thought he might have said, *How do you do.*

"Yes, as in, investments? Property? Mining?" he snapped.

I was taken aback by his tone. "Err, I have a cupcake store."

Benedict's response was to look out the porthole. As I had no suitable response, I did too, until my view was obscured by a well-dressed woman who walked over to Benedict and handed him some coffee. She leaned forward to shake my hand, rather a limp handshake. "Hello, I'm Laura Lindsey." She looked at me with clear distaste.

"Have you been to the island before, as well?" I asked her. When she inclined her head slightly, I added, "I'm going for the Beginners' Class. Surely you're not doing the Beginners' Class again like Lisa, or have I got the dates wrong?"

The two women looked at each other and smiled. Laura was the first to speak. "I always come to the island for a holiday to get away from my husband." She threw back her head and laughed. "I mean, he likes me to take cooking classes, but truth be told, I'm only going for rest and relaxation. Of course, I don't need to learn to cook, because we have staff for that. Every time I come, I repeat the Beginners' Class, because it's so much less effort."

The other woman nodded in agreement. "I've heard it's a small class," I said, "so how many others are there?"

"I've heard they usually keep the classes to about eight," Benedict said, turning his nose skyward. "I myself have never been to Paradise Island. I'm looking forward to the experience. I have, however, read about it, and I want to see if what I've read is accurate."

"It's only a small island," Laura said. "In fact, the cooking school is the only building on the island. There are no villages or other resorts, so it's completely private. It's far too small for a plane to land. Actually, it's quite a tiny island. The passenger boat goes twice a week, so the others will already be there. I'd say Mandy will be there. Mandy Martin. She's a regular. Mandy's father founded the famous investment firm, *Martins*, you know?"

I didn't know, but I nodded anyway. I was surprised that people took the Beginners' Class more than once. Still, going by what Laura had said, they appeared to have reasons other than cooking for going to the island. And judging by the predatory way she was looking at Benedict, I was beginning to have a good idea of just what those reasons might be.

I sipped my coffee and once more stared out to sea. There was nothing but sea and the curvature of the earth—there was no sign of land whatsoever. While I found it pleasant and relaxing, I was more than a little apprehensive about the school. After all, my cooking had improved, but that wasn't saying much. I would hate to be expelled from the cooking school and sent home in disgrace.

After another hour and a half, land came into view, much to my relief. I had become bored sitting there on the gently rocking boat. I considered myself lucky that I hadn't been seasick. As the boat drew closer to the island, I could see that Laura had been right. It was indeed a tiny island. I had once visited Daydream Island which was also in the Whitsundays, and thought it was small, and this island was about the same size. The island was more or less flat at the front, but the back of it rose to a sharp, albeit low, peak. It was no doubt an extinct volcano. I hoped it stayed extinct for the term of my visit.

The boat pulled into the jetty at a jagged outcrop of rocks, not quite the sandy beach I was expecting. Lisa must have followed my gaze. "Don't worry, Amelia. I know it doesn't look very nice from here, but there's a beautiful sandy beach in front of the building just over there." She pointed to her left.

When I stepped onto dry land, or to be precise, the wooden jetty with steel rails, I nearly tripped over the suitcases that someone had deposited there. There was quite a long walkway in front of me, and in the middle of it stood a man next to a huge trolley on wheels. He abandoned his trolley and hurried over to us. "Laura, Lisa, lovely to see you again!" he said loudly, although his expression said otherwise. He reached for my hand and then Benedict's, and shook each in turn vigorously. "You must be Amelia Spelled, and you must be Benedict Fletcher. Welcome to Paradise Island. I hope you enjoy your stay. Now please go ahead. The others are waiting, and I'll bring up your suitcases. I'm Owen. I own Paradise Island with my wife, Abby. We're all on first names here. Abby and I teach, along with our chef, Marcel." With that, he reached for the nearest suitcase, while the rest of us started our walk along the long winding pathway.

When the pathway took a sharp turn to the left, I gasped with delight at the vista before me. Lush plantings and manicured lawns stretched out to the pristine white beach and sparkling turquoise sea. A breathtaking wooden building sat snugly amongst coconut and palm trees in an elevated position above the sea.

The humidity was more intense on land, but the sea breeze lessened the effect somewhat. I inhaled the salt air and smiled.

"That's the Paradise Island Cooking School where we'll be staying," Laura said, somewhat unnecessarily.

I clasped my hands together. "It's beautiful!"

A woman was waiting for us on the vast deck. I looked past her at the tables with umbrellas that dotted the area in front of the beach. This was indeed paradise—I could stay here forever. The woman waited silently until we reached her, the scent of her elegant French perfume preceding her. She had a scowl on her face, which I thought very strange for someone running a business, but she smiled just before she spoke. "Welcome, all of you. You must be Amelia and Benedict."

We confirmed that we were. She was the least friendly female I had met that day, although she was civil enough. I wondered if she had been a model in her youth. She was tall, elegantly dressed, and was laden down with what appeared to be expensive jewellery. "My husband will take your suitcases to your rooms now," she said, followed by a further "*Now*, Owen!" to her unfortunate husband who was wheeling the trolley past us just at that moment.

"The maids won't be returning until tomorrow, so the complimentary cleaning service and the complimentary same day wash and press service won't be available until then. I hope this doesn't cause anyone any inconvenience." She gestured down the slope. "Feel free to use the pool at any time."

We all turned to look at the pool, and the half-naked man standing there waved to us. Lisa and I waved back. I wasn't looking at his six-pack, mind you. Truly.

"That's only the pool boy," Abby said derisively. "He cleans the pool."

"Imagine that!" The words were out of my mouth before I could stop them.

Abby shot me a sharp look before continuing. "Let me show you all to your rooms, and then please meet me out here for refreshments as soon as you've cleaned up. You can meet the others, and then we'll have our introductory cooking lesson."

"What?" I shrieked. "So soon?"

Abby frowned. "The classes proper start tomorrow, but we always have a little introductory lesson on the first day so we can all get to know each other over cooking. It's only something very simple, chocolate chip cookies."

Easy for you to say, I thought. I would have been happy to lie on the beach all day and never set foot inside the kitchen.

On a brighter note, my room was out of this world. It was breathtakingly magnificent, a huge bed on a beautiful, polished wooden floor. A couch backed onto the bed and afforded, through sliding doors, expansive views of the white sand with waves gently lapping. There was an outdoor setting and three beautiful palm trees behind it. A table to one side of the couch was laden with fresh fruit, wine, and chocolates.

It all screamed luxury. I poked my head into the en-suite bathroom and was surprised to see it was almost as big as the other room. A magnificent freestanding bath stood under double aspect windows over which were plantation shutters, and then off to one side were double vanities, each with their own mirror. It could only be more perfect if Alder had been here to share it with me. I thought how lovely it was for my friends to pay for this, considering it must have come at a high price.

I took photos of the room on my phone to send to Alder, but there was no service. I sure hoped there would be service at some time. The brochure stated there was WiFi, so I would have thought there would be mobile phone service, too.

I took a quick shower—I would languish in the bath later—and hurried out to the deck to meet the others.

When I arrived, Benedict was already deep in conversation with Laura. They both looked up at me. Was that guilt I could see on their faces?

Owen and Abby arrived immediately afterwards, accompanied by a tall, pinched-faced woman, as well as a woman who looked very much like Nigella Lawson. For a moment, I wondered if I had fallen into a themed celebrity look-alike event.

My eyes wandered to Benedict, and I was surprised to see that he had gone deathly white. He staggered to his feet and grasped the back of the chair. "Victoria!" he said in horror.

The woman likewise appeared horrified. "If you mean Victoria Vincent, then no, I'm her sister Vanessa." Her voice held a measure of distress.

I was shocked that she was English, given that I had thought she looked like Nigella Lawson.

"Vanessa?" Benedict said, taking a step closer and peering at her. "Pleased to meet you. I was devastated to hear of your sister's accident."

Vanessa dabbed at her eyes. "Yes, I can hardly bring myself to talk about it."

"Was it her heart that caused the fall?"

Vanessa shook her head. "I don't think so. She was fine after the surgery. Her psychiatrist said she'd been talking of suicide for the months leading up to her death. It all came out at the inquest."

"And this is Sarah, Sarah Stafford," Abby said loudly, obviously trying to break the sombre mood that had descended on the group. "And Mandy

Martin. Now we're just missing Michael Marshall."

Right on cue, a man hurried over to the group. "Sorry I'm late. Hello everyone!"

I took an instant liking to the man. He appeared to be in his fifties and had a decidedly cheerful manner.

As the others chatted amongst themselves, I wondered how I would remember everyone's names. Benedict, the English gentleman, was easy enough because he looked like Benedict Cumberbatch. I would remember Vanessa, because she too was English and looked like Nigella Lawson. I would remember Laura because she had a crush on Benedict, or so I thought.

I looked around at the others. I figured I would remember Michael, the cheerful man, because he was older than everyone else in the group. Owen, the owner, was clearly henpecked by his wife and bore a remarkable physical resemblance to Owen from *The Vicar of Dibley*. It was the other three women I was worried I'd mix up: Abby, Lisa, and Sarah. The three women did look very much like Laura, but Laura was never far from Benedict and was always staring up at him longingly. I didn't think I was in any danger of confusing Laura with anyone. She would be the one closest to Benedict.

Owen's announcement snapped me out of my reverie. "Please follow me to the teaching kitchen so we can have our introductory lesson. I always think baking is such an intimate thing, don't you?"

A choking noise sounded directly behind me.

CHAPTER 3

I swung around to see Abby pulling a rude face at her husband's remark. She avoided my gaze and pushed past me to cross the deck. It was with great trepidation that I followed her into the kitchen. It was, as was to be expected, a huge professional kitchen, all stainless steel and shiny surfaces, yet it did not have a clinical feel, far from it.

At any rate, kitchens always filled me with horror. I took careful note of the position of all the fire extinguishers, as well as the nearest exit. Owen directed us to sit on green and white metal seats at a long kitchen island facing the cooking area. That was the only splash of colour in the room, apart from the green feature wall behind the cooktops and ovens. The floors were a timber colour although I wasn't sure of their material, given that they did not look like real timber, and everything else was stainless steel with white countertops. The ceilings were quite high, and pendant lights hung low from them. The rest of the lighting was bright fluorescent even though it was a sunny afternoon.

Owen introduced the only person I had not yet met, a short, cranky-looking man. "This is Marcel de Vries," he announced proudly. "He's our French chef. He's been working for us for nine years, ever since we opened the Paradise Island Cooking School. Now as you already know, we keep the numbers low so students can work in small groups and then enjoy their cooking at a sit-down meal together afterwards. Today, Chef will show you how to make chocolate chip cookies. It's a nice way for everyone to get to know each other, and then the cooking classes proper will start tomorrow morning, bright and early."

I looked longingly out at the water lapping gently at the sand at the bottom of the slope. I wished I could be out there to dip my toes in the water instead of what I suspected was shortly to be the instigator of an insurance claim.

The chef spoke very quickly with a thick

French accent, and waved his arms around like a windmill as he spoke. I didn't quite follow what he was saying, but he did say that chocolate chip cookies should be chewy in the middle. My heart sank to my stomach. I was happy with my last baking effort because the edges of the cupcakes weren't rock hard. There was no way I would be able to make something soft in the middle. Come to think of it, I didn't even know if 'chewy in the middle' meant 'soft in the middle.' I supposed I was about to find out.

The chef bent over the fridge and then with a flourish, produced butter. "Take unsalted butter straight from the fridge," he said excitedly. "And now, there is brown sugar for caramel flavour which gives it the edge and white sugar for crunch." He demonstrated as he spoke. He moved rapidly, and I forgot everything as soon as he said it. Yes, I know he would give us a written recipe, but just the thought of baking made my mind go blank. It was on a par with doing taxes.

I shot a look at the others, but they weren't watching the chef. I supposed this was all second nature to them. Abby was deep in conversation with Michael Marshall, and kept touching his arm at intervals. Her husband, Owen, was likewise deep in conversation, but with Mandy. Benedict and Laura were playing footsies, and making no attempt to hide it. I wondered if the cooking school was in actuality a front for a Swingers' Club. I hoped no one thought I was a likely player!

The chef did not seem to mind that no one appeared overly interested in his cooking, but that was likely because he was so engrossed in what he was saying that he hadn't noticed what anyone else was doing. "Start at a low speed until it comes together and then start to increase the power," he said in his same rapid speech. "You can see how the butter and sugar ingredients have creamed together. Add eggs and a little bit of milk and then whisk it around until they are combined."

I tried to concentrate, but my heart was racing and my cortisol levels were out of control. Cooking always brought out the worst in me. The fact that he said, "You need to be precise when you're baking," just made matters worse.

As he said something unintelligible followed by, "Two cups of plain flour and make sure they're level," I could sense my blood pressure skyrocketing.

I leaned forward and forced myself to concentrate. "Now it's very important to get this part right," he said. "Use one quarter teaspoon of baking powder, one quarter of a teaspoon of baking soda, and one quarter of a teaspoon of salt." His hands moved so rapidly that my eyes had trouble following him.

Just then, a loud text sound emanated from my pocket. I pulled out my phone and turned off the sound as I mumbled my apologies. I surreptitiously looked at the screen. The text was from Alder, but before I could read it, Benedict barked at me. "It is not polite to have one's phone turned on during a cooking class."

"That's right!" Sarah snapped. "How rude."

I wanted to say something cutting, but instead apologised. "I thought there was no service," I added. "I tried earlier and couldn't get a call or a message out."

Abby waved my concerns away. "That's quite all right. There *is* good service here most times, but there's a storm on the way. That usually plays havoc with the service."

The chef, clearly oblivious to others speaking around him, continued. "And now to the chocolate. Use top quality eating dark chocolate. *Non*! Not the for-cooking chocolate! Eehh-arghh! Cut it with a knife like this"—he demonstrated in the manner of a serial killer with a hapless victim —"so you have different shapes and textures, some big pieces, some little pieces, some shards. Make sure you cut it up finely enough, as you don't want large chunks. Good quality chocolate will stay soft when it's baked."

That's what you think! I thought. *Wait 'til you try my cooking.* I shuddered.

And now to the part I was dreading. The chef declared that we should make our own cookies, and that he, Owen, and Abby would oversee our efforts. I was glad at the promise of help, but to my dismay, none eventuated. Owen helped Mandy, and Abby helped Michael. The chef appeared fixated on Vanessa. The rest of us were left to our own devices.

I did the best I could by copying the others, until Sarah noticed and glared at me. Abby appeared to notice my incompetence, as she occasionally called out instructions such as, "Fold that into the mixture," followed by "No, not like that," several times.

The chef then returned to the front. "Now scoop the mixture onto your baking tray just so, remembering that the mixture will spread. Make each precisely the same size. Yes, and now place the trays into the oven for twelve minutes."

It was the longest twelve minutes of my life. I kept one eye on the oven and one eye on the closest fire extinguisher.

To my surprise, the twelve minutes passed uneventfully, and we were told to take our cookies from the oven and place them on the cooling racks. I was delighted that the cookies were not black and the cooling rack did not collapse, just buckled. There was no fire. This was indeed a significant improvement.

The chef walked up and down, peering at the cookies. When he reached mine, he said, "They should be crunchy on the outside and golden brown on the base. These cookies should not be hard all the way through." He glowered at me, and I wondered how he knew they were hard all the way through just by looking at them. He then spoke to Vanessa in French for a good five minutes, while the rest of us stood around awkwardly.

"And now that they are cool, we shall make them into s'mores," the chef said. "We shall do this again later in the week around a campfire on the beach. Place marshmallows on one half, and a slab of dark chocolate on the other."

I inhaled the delightful aroma of sugary caramel on top of the marshmallows.

"Now take one side and place on top of the other side," the chef said. "You need to eat s'mores quickly. I shall sample one of each student's."

My whole body tensed at that. Vanessa's was first. "Well done! A sticky indulgence!" the chef exclaimed with delight. "You were not good at cutting the chocolate, but no matter; this is superb!" He then reached for mine, and I instinctively took a step backwards.

He placed one of my s'mores in his mouth and bit down hard. Simultaneously, his eyes widened. He clutched at his throat and then screamed, a horrible, high-pitched scream. As he did so, something hard fell to the ground and clattered away.

He threw himself at me, yelling rapid-fire words in French.

Owen and Michael grabbed him before he reached me. He covered his mouth and continued to yell in French. I saw that Vanessa's face had turned bright red.

"It's his front teeth," Abby said in horror. "They're missing!"

"No, they're not," Michael said calmly, as he

bent down to pick something off the ground. "Here they are. If he goes to a dentist quickly, the teeth can be put back in."

"Hurry, the boat hasn't left yet," Abby said urgently. "Take him to the boat! Hurry up, Owen!"

Owen escorted the furious chef from the room, while I apologised profusely to Abby. "Don't worry about it," Michael said, patting me on the shoulder. "It could happen to anyone. By the way, you can't speak French, can you?" I shook my head. "Good, good," he added.

"I'm so sorry, I've ruined everything," I said sadly. "Now there's no chef."

Abby threw my cookies in the trash. "No need to worry," she said in a tone that was clearly worried. "Owen and I are chefs, so the classes will continue as usual. They're the Beginners' Classes after all, not the French Patisserie classes. Why don't you all relax until dinner, which will be served at six in the dining room. Feel free to wander around."

I was the first to leave the room, my cheeks burning. I was mortified. I barely breathed again until I was in my room. I locked the door and leaned against it. Oh gosh, I knew this wasn't a good idea. I crossed to the bed and reached for the remote. No reception. A look out the window showed me why. The clear blue skies had been replaced by threatening black clouds, and the sea was wild. I could almost smell the coming storm in the air.

It was then I remembered that Alder had texted me. I swiped the screen to read his message. *Amelia, get off the island fast! I did a divination and you're in danger!*

CHAPTER 4

*E*very muscle in my body tensed. I hurried to the sliding door and opened it, only to see the boat sailing off to sea. I was stuck on the island, and the next boat wouldn't be here for days. I tried to text Alder, but again there was no service. I at once connected my phone to the charger. If the coming storm cut the power, I didn't want to be without a charged phone if danger was headed for me.

I sat on the bed and forced myself to think rationally. Who would have reason to harm me? The only one who came to mind was the chef, and he was on the boat on its way to the mainland. Or would I be in danger from the storm? I knew the area had frequent bad storms, but there was no reason to think that the coming storm would be worse than any other.

Hopefully, Alder would send more information, but until he did, I would just have to be vigilant and take precautions. Luckily I had brought my travel altar. I crossed to my suitcase and rummaged through it for my little bag of supplies and discovered the jar I was looking for near the top. It held a mixture of cascarilla powder and red brick dust. I unscrewed the bottle and sprinkled the substance across my doorway and the sliding doors, and then across the two windows in the bathroom.

One of the shutters blew inwards as I did so, bringing with it a gust of sea air. I fastened it shut, and shivered. The air was fairly alive with electric current, and the storm was gathering momentum. I hurried back to my bag, retrieved two bay leaves, and placed one in each shoe as fast as I could. Now, what other protective measures did I have? I checked my phone again, but still no service. Energy was building, and I knew it was more than the storm. Why would I be in danger? Perhaps Owen and Abby wanted to do away with me because I had proven to all and sundry that I was a terrible cook, but would that be any reason to murder me? I supposed that depended on just how seriously they took food.

After checking the locks on the doors and the latches on the windows, I threw myself back on the bed. I intended to close my eyes just for a minute to try to relax.

When I awoke, it was dark, or dusk, to be precise. I leaped out of bed and checked my phone —still no service, but to my dismay, it was just after six. Did they dress for dinner? I had no idea, but I quickly pulled a lilac and white dress over my head and strapped on some heels. I again stuck a bay leaf in each shoe, and dabbed some Fiery Wall of Protection Oil on the back of my neck.

I followed my nose to the dining room from which emanated the heady scent of dukkah spices. The interior was sophisticated and stylish with huge windows overlooking the sea. I could certainly get used to this lifestyle. The décor was tropical and beachy, as was to be expected. My eye went straight to a giant Buddha next to a stunning wall feature. This was indeed a tropical oasis.

Everyone else was sitting around a long rectangular glass and timber table, and I took my seat on a beautifully textured seagrass woven chair.

"Sorry I'm late," I said. "I fell asleep."

"You're not late at all," Michael said kindly, although Benedict pointedly looked at his watch and cleared his throat loudly.

Sarah pouted at me. "To the contrary, she *is* late, and it's inconvenienced us all."

Benedict nodded his approval at her. "You're a journalist, aren't you?" When she said that she was, he added, "I might just have a big scoop for you later."

Owen, who was sitting at the end of the table, stood up. "A tropical storm is on its way." He held up his hand. "Now there's no need to be alarmed. Tropical storms are not uncommon in this area, and we're well set up for them. It will sound wild, and the windows will shake, but there's nothing to worry about. The worst that will happen is that the mobile phone service and the internet won't come back on until the storm blows over. We have a large generator, and the cooking and hot water are gas. Obviously, you shouldn't go outside when the storm comes, but here inside, you won't notice it."

"Then why are there candles on the table?" Benedict said. "There seem to be more candles than warranted, if you are simply trying to set up an ambience."

Owen appeared to be quite taken aback at the remark. "If the power goes out, obviously I'll have to go outside and flip the power over to the generator," he explained. "During that time, there'll be no lights or power at all, so it's surely common sense to have candles burning as a precaution."

Benedict glared at him, but I was more concerned about the prospect of the lights going out. If someone wanted to harm me, then a dark room would be the perfect place to do so. I needed to keep my wits about me, and for this reason I had declined the wine.

Abby stood up and nodded to her husband, who promptly sat down. "Please bear with us. We're several staff members down, but that doesn't mean we can't continue as usual. After tonight, we will prepare each meal in the teaching kitchen, as usual. Because of the storm, the maids won't be able to come tomorrow on the staff boat that passes by our island, and that will be the only inconvenience."

The meal proved to be delicious, but the conversation was tense. Benedict continued to make snide remarks, which no one, apart from Laura, appeared to appreciate. He complained about the meal several times, and each time Owen's face grew redder. Abby didn't appear to mind, engrossed as she was with Michael.

"Vanessa, you look very like your sister," Benedict said in a snarky tone.

Vanessa simply glared at him and did not respond. She was visibly upset by his remark. I thought it quite cruel of him to mention Vanessa's deceased sister.

"You know, you're…" he continued, addressing Vanessa once more, but he was interrupted by Owen.

"You're Benedict Fletcher!" he said, standing abruptly.

Benedict laughed softly. "Of course I am. That is the name under which I have booked, is it not?" Laura laughed, too.

Owen's cheeks puffed with anger. "You're the famous food critic!"

Benedict smirked.

"How dare you come to our resort!"

Abby pulled on Owen's sleeve, but he paid no attention. "You've ruined the reputation of many a cooking school with your nasty remarks." Abby tugged on Owen's sleeve harder, but he wrenched his arm away in what I guessed was a rare show of disobedience.

A supercilious expression swamped Benedict's face. "Indeed, my article will be truly *interesting* this time. I shall comment on the amiable manner of the host and on the *quality* of the food, as well as the *extra-curricular* activities." He said the word 'quality' with derision. "I hardly came under false pretences."

Owen approached Benedict's chair in a belligerent manner. "I wasn't expecting a famous food critic to come to Australia!"

Benedict appeared unperturbed by Owen's proximity. "I'm conducting a tour of Australian cooking schools for my new book. I've heard a lot about your cooking school, and I'm here to see if the rumours are true."

"But you'll ruin us!" Owen said loudly, just as the windows shook in a sudden gust of wind.

Abby, clearly alarmed, hurried to position herself between the two men.

Benedict threw down his napkin with a flourish. "I am leaving!" he said as he stood. "Good night." He hurried from the room.

The lights flickered and thunder boomed simultaneously. Abby turned to her husband.

"Owen, we should serve dessert. *Now!*" They cleared the table and scurried from the room, whispering to each other. I clearly caught the words, 'ruin us' about five times.

More thunder and lightning accompanied their departure.

Laura pushed back her chair. "I'm scared of thunderstorms. I'll go to my room. Goodnight. Please make my apologies to our hosts."

I wondered if it was as plain to everyone else as it was to me exactly where she was headed—directly to Benedict's room. I didn't think there was much doubt, but it was none of my business.

"Are you all right?" Lisa asked Vanessa, who was furiously rubbing her temples.

Vanessa shook her head. "I have the beginnings of a headache. Nothing to worry about." We all then sat in uncomfortable silence until Owen and Abby returned.

"Sorry we took so long," Abby said when they finally did return, carrying desserts. "We were just, um…" Her voice trailed away. She deposited a heavenly looking dessert in front of me. "Caramelised lemon saffron tart with torched meringue. You'll all learn how to make it later in the week."

That was encouraging. I thought I would be good at torching the meringue—if I survived, that is. I still couldn't imagine the type of danger I was in. Benedict was the only one so far to have made enemies. I would be careful to stay away from windows and doors in case the storm uprooted a tree and blew it inside the building. I had seen every *Final Destination* movie, so I wasn't taking any chances.

When everyone had been served, Mandy said, "I forgot to charge my phone. Please excuse me, I'll be right back."

Owen stood up once more. "I forgot the flashlights. The electricity usually becomes intermittent in a storm, so please keep a flashlight with you during night hours." His words were punctuated by such a loud clap of thunder that everybody jumped.

I had finished my dessert by the time he came back with the flashlights, and none too soon, as the lights were now flickering consistently.

"What took you so long?" Abby snapped.

"Just cleaning up," he muttered.

Mandy returned to the table. "Oh, I'm so sorry, everyone's finished their delicious dessert already. I got sidetracked and lost all track of time." She immediately tucked into her dessert.

Owen rapidly ate his dessert, and then checked that all the flashlights were working. He took the batteries out of the only one that he said didn't work properly and fiddled with them for ages. Abby was visibly annoyed. "I'll clear the table while you're doing that," she snapped. "Would anyone like coffee?"

We all said that we would. Michael offered to help Abby, as did Lisa, but Abby declined her offer of help.

"We would usually have our coffee in another room," Abby said when she and Michael had served everyone the coffee, "but the storm's getting quite wild and it's best if we stay together at this table with all the candles."

Just then, the lights went out. I reached for my flashlight, and then froze. I was relieved to see that the candles provided sufficient light to see everyone. In fact, they provided more illumination than I had thought they would.

"Don't worry," Owen said. "The lights will probably come back on soon, so let's just wait and see. I won't go out to the generator house unless it's clear that they'll stay off."

Vanessa stood up abruptly. "I'll have to go and

take some Advil," she said. "Then I'll come back and enjoy my coffee."

The storm outside was wild, so wild that I thought the roof might come crashing in. I had never experienced a tropical storm before, but I took comfort in the fact that Owen and Abby had experienced many and did not appear the least bit concerned.

Lisa rubbed her arms. "I'm getting a little chilly," she said. "I'll just go to my room and get my wrap. I'll be right back."

With that, she too disappeared from the room. I wondered if she was coming down with the flu, because it was anything but chilly. Still, I was used to a cold climate and these people were likely used to the tropics.

I had finished my coffee by the time Vanessa returned. "Where's Lisa?" she demanded to know.

I shrugged. "I'm sure she's coming back. She said she was just going to get her wrap."

"How long has she been gone?" Vanessa asked imperiously.

"She left just after you did." I had no idea why it was so important to Vanessa.

Lisa walked in at that moment, but Vanessa barely looked at her.

I wondered if Vanessa was going to demand fresh coffee, when a torrential gust of wind blew the shutters open with considerable force, and the candles went out.

CHAPTER 5

I was terrified. I heard, but did not see, at least one person running in the direction of the windows, and I heard the shutters slam shut. The howling in the room stopped, but the lights did not come back on. Just then, everyone in the room must have remembered their flashlights, because we all turned them on at once.

"It's quite wild out there," Owen said in something of an understatement. "I'll just pop out to the generator shed and switch over to the generator."

The rest of us sat at the table while the walls shook. The howling was now clearly audible in the room.

"This is just a typical tropical storm," Abby

said calmly. "Please don't be alarmed. It will all pass by morning, or in a day or two."

A day or two? Surely she couldn't be serious.

"Anyway," she continued, "we should all stay together until Owen gets the power back on. I know you all have flashlights, but it's safer to wait for the power. The resort is set up for storms such as this, so when you return to your rooms, make sure that all the shutters are firmly latched. I'm sure I don't need to tell you not to go outside until we give you the all clear."

We all murmured our agreement.

"I hope Benedict and Laura are all right," Michael said.

Abby nodded. "If they have any concerns, I'm sure they'll come out and speak to us."

"But they don't have flashlights," Michael pointed out.

Right then, the room reverberated violently, whether from the boom of thunder that had just cracked overhead or the gale-force wind, I had no idea.

Michael stood up. "I should go and check on them."

Abby nodded. "Thanks, Michael. Here, take my flashlight and this spare one, and give them one each. Benedict's room is quite close. It's the closest room to the staff kitchen, number eight."

The lights came on for a second and then went off just as Michael reached the far side of the room. I took it as a good sign that Owen was getting the generator working. I put my flashlight down on the table, and realised that all my muscles were tense. I made a concerted effort to relax, but, try as I might, I could not get Alder's text out of my mind.

The shutters were now banging in a constant rhythm, and the howling wind outside sounded like something out of an old horror movie.

To my relief, the lights came back on, and did not flicker. Just as they did, Michael burst back into the room. His face was white and ashen and he was clutching his throat. Abby raced to him. "Whatever's wrong, Michael?"

My first thought was that he was having a heart attack, and I wondered what would happen to him, considering the storm had stranded us on the island.

He pointed over his shoulder and tried to speak. We all left our seats and hurried over to him. "Benedict, Laura, Benedict, Laura," he stuttered.

"Are they all right?" Abby asked him.

He shook his head. "No."

Abby pushed past him and hurried down the hall, with the rest of us hard on her heels. Benedict's door was open.

Abby was the first in the room, and I heard her gasp. I stuck my head around the door. Benedict was lying on his back with a large kitchen knife protruding from his chest, and Laura was in his bed. She, too, had been impaled with a kitchen knife.

I averted my eyes from the gruesome scene and stepped back into the corridor. The others did likewise. Michael, who appeared to have recovered quickly, took charge of the situation.

"Abby, do you have the key to this room?"

Abby stared ahead, her eyes glazed. Michael shook her gently and repeated the question.

"There's a master key in the office." Her voice trembled.

"Okay, you go and get it and then come back here."

After Abby left, the others spoke, but all their words merged into mumbo jumbo to my ears. All were expressing surprise, wondering who could have done such a thing, but no-one commented on the fact that Laura was in Benedict's bed. Their relationship must have been obvious to everyone.

I was dumbstruck. My first thought was that the murderer was standing, if not only feet away from me, then elsewhere on the island. The storm had isolated all of us, so unless there was someone on the island I did not know about, the murderer was either Abby or Owen, one of the guests, or the pool boy. The only person I could rule out with any certainty was myself. I leaned back against the doorpost for support.

Abby returned and made to lock the door, but Michael stopped her. "The police won't be able to get to the island until the storm blows over, so we need to take photographs of the crime scene. I'll do that now."

He pulled his phone from his pocket and went back into the room. I assumed he was taking photos with his phone, but I had no wish to watch. That was a sight I would never forget, and I did not want to see it a second time.

I had forgotten about Owen, until he appeared in the corridor. He was drenched. "What's going on?" He looked genuinely surprised, so unless he was a good actor, perhaps I could rule him out as the perpetrator.

Michael came straight to the point. "Benedict and Laura have been murdered."

Owen's jaw dropped. "What?"

When no one said anything else, Owen marched into the room. He wasn't in there long before he emerged white and shaken. "But who, who?"

No one had any response. Michael was the first to speak. "Owen, you and I should remove the bodies to the cool room, while Abby can take the ladies back to the dining room."

"The cool room?" Mandy asked.

Michael nodded. "The police won't be able to come until the storm blows over, so we can't preserve the crime scene as it is. I suggest Owen and I take the bodies to the cool room, and then lock the door to preserve the crime scene as best we can for when the police actually do get here."

I was grateful for his quick thinking.

"Actually, someone should stay at the door while we're taking the, err, bodies to the cool room," Michael added, "just so any evidence in there won't be tampered with."

"Who would tamper with any evidence?" Sarah asked.

"Why, the murderer of course," Michael said.

Mandy gasped, but he pressed on. "That's why I suggest you all stay together, perhaps just down the corridor, to make sure no one goes into the room."

"I've had an awful shock," Sarah said haughtily. "I need to go and sit down. I need a brandy."

Michael agreed. "That should be all right, but I insist at least three women remain."

I knew where he was going with that statement. He suspected more than one person might be involved in the murder.

Abby led us to the end of the corridor and we all studiously looked the other way while Owen and Michael took the bodies out of the room one by one. As soon as they had left with the second body, Abby hurried back and locked the door. "Come on ladies, I think we all need a strong drink."

I had to admire her. Her voice was shaking, but she was doing her best not to show that she was scared.

When we joined Sarah at the dining table, Abby lit the candles.

"Surely the power won't go out again?" Sarah snapped.

Abby shook her head. "I'm sure it won't, but I'm not taking any chances."

I checked my phone out of habit. No service, but then again I hadn't expected any.

"Amelia," Abby said, "there won't be any service here in the storm."

"How will you call the police?" Vanessa spoke for the first time since the discovery of the body.

Owen, who just then was returning to the room with Michael, answered her. "That's just it. I don't know if we *can* call them."

"You obviously can't, you silly man," Sarah snapped. "There *is* no mobile service. We're stranded here all alone on a desert island and one of us is a murderer!" She burst into hysterical tears.

I didn't know whether to point out that it was a tropical island, not a desert island, or to slap her across her face to cure her hysteria. I wanted to do both, but in the end, I did neither, much to my regret.

"There's usually service at the top of the hill," Owen said evenly.

I spoke up. "Do you mean the mountain?" I thought of the hill I had seen upon my arrival that looked like a volcano covered with dense vegetation.

"It's just a hill," Owen said. "Even in the worst storm, we can usually get intermittent service up the top."

"But isn't it too dangerous to go outside in the storm?" I asked him.

"We have two tunnels," Owen said, "quite big tunnels that were built many years ago, no doubt by pirates. The tunnels don't continue all the way to the top of the hill, but they do go most of the way, and we will only be outside when we're going the short distance from the end of one tunnel to the start of the other."

"Who is this *we*?" Lisa asked him.

"Michael and I have just had a conversation about it, and we think we all need to stick together."

Sarah pulled her hands from her eyes. "You're afraid the murderer is going to pick us off one by one, aren't you?" Her tone was still hysterical.

Michael shook his head. "I'm afraid there's no nice way to put this, so I'll come straight to the point. As you've said, this island is now cut off from the outside world. Yet someone murdered those two people. It's one of us."

"What about the pool boy?" I asked him.

"He went on the boat yesterday," Michael said. "He was supposed to come back tomorrow on the staff boat that goes past here to the next group of islands."

"There's no one else living on the island?" I asked Owen.

Abby answered for him. "No, the island's too small for that."

The others fell silent for a moment, no doubt trying to digest, as I was, that one of us was a cold blooded killer.

"It's dark now," Michael said, "so I don't think we should risk going to the top of the hill to call the police tonight. Let's all go to our rooms and then meet back here in the morning to try to get a call out to the authorities."

"Who exactly will be going up to the hill?" Sarah asked.

Owen and Michael exchanged glances. "We'll decide tomorrow," Owen said. "Abby and I will escort you all to your rooms now. I think you'll all agree that no one should be alone, that is, outside your own rooms. Make sure the doors are locked, and don't open your door to anyone, no matter what. We should all meet back here in the dining room at seven."

I didn't think it was the best idea, splitting up like that, but I couldn't think of a suitable alternative.

After Abby and Owen walked me to my room, I rapidly locked the door behind me, and then with my key still in hand looked under my bed and behind the couch. I sprinted to the bathroom and searched it for murderers, and then hurried out to the bedroom to look in the dresser drawers. Sure, it would have to be a short, emaciated murderer, but one cannot be too careful with a murderer on the loose.

I checked the sliding door was latched, and then went back to look at the bathroom windows. I wondered what else I could do to make the area secure. I could pull the bed across the door, but that would still leave the sliding door area exposed. I decided there was no point.

If the power went out again, at least I had the flashlight, and I had also brought several tea light candles in case I needed to do spells.

When I sat on the bed, I realised my knees were shaking. I was tired, but I was scared. I checked my phone again, but there was still no service. I'd have to make sure that I was one of the people to go up the hill the next day. I had to get a call through to Alder to tell him what had happened. I knew he'd be worried that he hadn't heard back from me, and I hoped he was doing spells to keep me safe. I knew Thyme, Ruprecht, Camino, and Mint would be worried, too, and would no doubt realise I was in need of protection. The thought gave me some small measure of comfort.

The wind blew wildly against the sliding doors. They continued to rattle violently, yet I could hardly hear them over the sound of my racing heart.

I sat on the bed and clutched the phone to me. I wanted Alder there, but his message would have to do. I tried to think through the situation rationally. Owen and Abby had run the Paradise Island Cooking School for the past nine years. Surely I would have heard if someone else had been murdered on the island, so that meant they weren't serial killers. That seemed logical. And if they had done away with Benedict, it was no doubt because they thought he would ruin their business. Perhaps Laura was collateral damage—wrong place, wrong time. If that was the case, and while it was entirely reprehensible, by my reasoning they were unlikely to murder anyone else.

Still, I couldn't shake the feeling that there was going to be another murder. I didn't feel safe locked in my room, and I didn't have any weapons. I was defenceless. I corrected myself. No, that was wrong. I was a Dark Witch. I was powerful.

So why didn't I feel powerful, as I sat huddled, clutching my knees to me with Alder's message in my lap, and jumping at every sound?

It was hours before I fell asleep. Sleep came only when I could fight it no longer. My last waking thought was that I hoped I wouldn't wake up dead.

CHAPTER 6

J did, in fact, wake up very much alive— as alive as anyone could be in a caffeine-deprived state. My first order of business was to do a protection spell. I was happy I had heeded Ruprecht's advice to prepare for every eventuality. I took out my jar of vinegar and sulphur and placed it in the middle of the room. I had already charged it by speaking a spell over it before I left for the island. This was an old method to drive away harm.

The storm had not abated; the rain pelted loudly and viciously against the sliding doors. I pulled back the curtain to look out, but could see nothing but a wall of water.

I carried two sticks of incense to the bathroom

and placed them in the bath. One was Dragon's Blood and the other was a combination of frankincense and myrrh. Together, the three made up Fiery Wall of Protection incense.

I put some comfrey root in my jeans pocket. It was for protection while travelling, and I would be travelling up the hill soon enough, or so I hoped. With that in mind, I wrote the names 'Abby,' 'Owen,' and 'Michael,' as they were the decision makers, on a piece of paper and under their names wrote, 'I am easily permitted to go up the hill whenever I want.' I added some sugar for sweetness, so that they would be sweetly disposed to me, and some calamus root and liquorice root for compulsion. Yes, I know it was a spell to get them to agree to allow me up the hill, but this could be a matter of life and death, and in my magical tradition, that is, eclectic traditional witchcraft with some borrowing from hoodoo, it wasn't an ethical dilemma at all. Not all witchcraft paths share the same views.

I took the Fiery Wall of Protection oil that was sitting on the dresser, and with it drew a large pentagram with my finger on the door and all the windows. I said the words as I did so: *With this pentagram I here write, protect me both day and night.*

I drew a pentagram on each mirror, while uttering the words;

Protection spell where you are set

Shall easily drive away all threat

All evil entering this place

Is driven backwards with all haste

I set this down and do agree

This is my will, so mote it be.

I placed a bay leaf at every corner of the bedroom and the bathroom. I checked my phone for service before I left the room—no luck as usual —and hurried down the corridor to the dining room.

"Am I late?" I said, upon seeing I was the last one to arrive.

"No," Abby said. "We all just got here early."

I did a quick head count and saw to my relief that everyone was present and accounted for. The life-saving aroma of coffee beckoned to me. I hurried over to pour myself a cup just as Abby spoke again. "We were just about to decide who should go up the hill and who should stay here."

Michael interrupted her. "And I was thinking that Owen should go up the hill with half the group, and I should stay here with Abby." When Owen raised his eyebrows, he pushed on. "Abby and Owen are the owners of the place and know the territory. I don't mean to be sexist, but Owen would be more capable of handling, shall we say, an intruder than Abby. If Abby stays in the building, then a man should stay with her."

"It makes sense to me," I said.

No one else disagreed. "I insist on going up the hill," Sarah snapped. "I get claustrophobia and anxiety, oh and nausea, from being locked in a room."

Nobody pointed out to her that the resort was hardly a room, but no one would be likely to disagree with her, given her temper.

"I want to go up the hill, too," I said firmly. "I'm very good at cross country running and hill climbing." It was a blatant lie, but to my surprise, nobody disagreed with me. It must have been the spell working.

It was all too easy in the end. It was settled that I would go up the hill with Owen, Sarah, and Vanessa, while Mandy, Lisa, Abby, and Michael stayed in the building.

Everyone appeared to be tense and shaken, as was to be expected when a double murder had occurred, and I supposed that no one would feel any better until the police arrived and took over, or better still, until we could get off the island. Everyone that is, except the murderer—or murderers. I had to accept the fact that more than one person might be involved. I had to keep myself safe until help arrived. Meanwhile, my best chance was to get a message to Alder, and if I had to climb a ghastly hill to do it, then so be it.

Vanessa and I followed Owen through the corridors of the resort, with Sarah following behind, complaining about everything imaginable. She was muttering about not wanting to go with Vanessa, but did not say why. I wanted to cut her some slack because we were all affected by the murder, but she was the only one carrying on like that. Besides, she was like it *before* the murders.

Owen came to a door which he unlocked. When we walked inside, I realised it was the office. At the back of the office was a particularly wide door. Owen crossed the room and opened it.

I was the second person through the door. I had expected another room, but this was the tunnel of which they had spoken. I was hit in the face with stale, musty air and the scent of something rank and unpleasant, perhaps a dead rat. My flashlight illuminated cobwebs, and I shuddered. I steeled myself to step inside. I really had no choice in the matter—I had to get a message to Alder.

"You'll need your flashlights in the tunnels," Owen explained unnecessarily. "There's no power to the tunnels. We never come in here. The last time anyone was in those tunnels was when I had to get a message out in the last bad storm."

I was concerned and more than a little frightened. I was going to walk along a dark tunnel with three people, and one or more of them could be a killer. I had to stop reminding myself of that fact, because it was setting my nerves on edge.

I shone my flashlight around, but tried to avoid shining it on cobwebs, and that was a little difficult as they were everywhere. The floor was dirt and the walls were made of brick. The mortar was crumbling and falling out in places. I then had the worrying thought that the tunnels might collapse, but consoled myself with the fact they had stood all this time and there was no sign of any collapse. The tunnel was sufficiently large to accommodate a tall person easily, and for that I was grateful. I don't know what I would have done if we had to crawl through a tunnel. I didn't think I would have been able to do that. My eyes started to adjust to the darkness, but that simply manifested as a murky, dim corona appearing around the flashlight beams.

"How long is this tunnel?" I asked Owen, puzzled because we were only rising slightly. I would have expected the tunnel to rise at once.

Before he could answer, Sarah and Vanessa had an argument. They had fallen behind, and I couldn't hear what they were saying.

"Hurry up and keep up, you two," Owen said. "It's not safe to lag behind." As both women hurried over to him, he answered my question. "This tunnel shortly brings us to the tunnel that climbs."

"Is it the same size as this tunnel?" I asked hopefully.

He hesitated before answering. "More or less."

I had, of course, heard the expression 'light at the end of the tunnel,' but I was pleased when I saw said light. Rather than how I had imagined it, as a well-defined speck of light that became larger and larger, the reality was that it appeared as a pale mist that grew with every step I took. The light played tricks with my eyes. First, I fancied I saw the silhouette of a giant black cat, and then the figure of a menacing man. I knew they were but shadows, but the sight filled me with the same dread I had felt as a young child hiding in my bed, watching the shadows play over my closet doors.

Owen motioned for us to stop. "When we come out of this tunnel, we have to make our way over the short distance to the opening of the next tunnel. The wind will be very strong, so take care not to be blown over."

We gathered at the entrance to the tunnel, and I noticed outside two axes stuck in a wood chopping block. I figured it was not the best idea to have two axes in the open when there was a murderer on the loose, and I was about to point this out to Owen, but he yelled "Follow me!" and sprinted from the tunnel.

The rain lashed out at me with fury as I approached the second tunnel's entrance. The sound of the storm's roaring was deafening. I could barely stand and I wondered how I would make it the short distance to the other tunnel.

I whipped around as Sarah screamed.

"Don't leave me alone with her!" Sarah shrieked, and then threw herself after Owen, with Vanessa hard on her heels. I was sure she was referring to Vanessa and not to me, but that was the least of my worries. Nothing had prepared me for the ferocity of the storm.

Palm leaves lashed across my face. The rain was so strong that I couldn't open my eyes properly, only squint to see where I was going. I could barely keep my footing, even though the dense foliage of the undergrowth protected me to some degree.

The other tunnel wasn't far, but by the time I reached it, I was drenched right through to the bone. My clothes clung tightly to me and my soaking jeans weighed me down. I stopped to catch my breath and to empty water from my shoes.

The others had fared no better. Sarah was already complaining at the top of her lungs. The normally unperturbed Owen turned beet red. "You're the one who insisted upon coming to the top of the hill," he reminded her, but far from imparting any sense of logic to her, his words set her off into a tirade of verbal abuse.

Vanessa and I exchanged glances. "Well then, let's be going," I said brightly, and forged ahead. I did it partly to stop Sarah's ranting, and also because I wanted to be at the front of the pack. In all the murder mystery movies I had seen in which people were walking in single file, the ones at the back were always murdered first.

We hadn't gone far before we encountered the

first set of steps. I had all but forgotten the spiders and the gloomy dark, due to my discomfort with my squelching shoes and soaked clothes. We climbed for some time in silence, although the silence was punctuated by Sarah's complaints.

Some of the steps were quite steep, but I was more concerned about being underground for so long. All in all, it was hard going. I could tell that Vanessa and Sarah were still behind me, not only by the pools of light from their flashlights, but by their heavy panting. Not that I was one to talk; this was quite a workout.

In some places, the tunnel narrowed, and I had to stoop, yet it was wide enough not to give me an attack of claustrophobia.

"The end of the tunnel is just up ahead," Owen said.

Never had I heard sweeter words. Once again, the unrelenting rain lashed me, but I wiped the rain from my eyes and peered eagerly ahead. Sarah pushed past me. "What's going on?" she screeched. "That's not the top of the hill!"

CHAPTER 7

I had to agree with her, and for a horrible moment I thought Owen had brought us here to kill us. This was not the top of a hill. In front of us was a wall of rocks.

Owen pointed to the top of the rocks. "Just up there!" He had to yell to be heard over the driving rain. "We just have to climb this rock face."

Sarah snorted rudely. "I can't climb that!" she screeched.

Owen merely walked away and I followed him. To my relief, there was a pathway behind the biggest rock and the area was sheltered by towering trees. It was narrow, but it was hardly rock climbing. I once again made sure I fell in just behind Owen as we climbed the short but steep trail to the top of the hill.

The top of the hill would have afforded a beautiful view in good weather, but now all I could see was a wall of grey rain, the only break in the vista being leaves as they were whipped viciously from trees.

I pressed my back against a small rock and sat down, so I could keep an eye on the other three and so no one could come up behind me. They were all intently staring at their phones, and I assumed Owen was trying to reach the police. I had already written a text to Alder. I pressed 'send' and held my breath as the little bar moved slowly across the screen. My hopes rose as the bar reached the side of the screen, but then the message came up, *Your message cannot be sent. Try again.*

I tried again. Same result as before. I repeated the process several times, sometimes looking up at Owen to see if he had managed to get through to the police, but given that he hadn't said a word, I supposed he hadn't.

As I pressed *Try again* for the umpteenth time, it sent, and I heard Owen's voice speaking urgently. Thank the goddess!

I tried to call Alder, but it went straight to voicemail. I left a rapid message, and then tried to call Thyme. Just as I did so, the service dropped out.

"I've told the police," Owen said. "Thank goodness for that!"

"How long before they can get here?" Vanessa asked him.

"Not until the storm stops, obviously," Owen said.

"She *obviously* is asking how long before the storm stops," Sarah said in a snarky tone.

"It seems to be dying down now," Owen said, "but I have no idea how long it will take before the police can get here."

I realised that the storm was indeed lessening. When I had run between the two tunnels, I had barely been able to stand, but we had climbed the rocks without the violent winds.

"The storm usually comes in cycles," Owen said, "so we had better get back before it picks up again."

On the way back down the rocky formation, which I found harder going down than up, a horrible thought occurred to me. What if Owen was the murderer, and hadn't really called the police? "Vanessa and Sarah, did either of you call the police?" I asked them.

"I was leaving that up to Owen," Vanessa said behind me.

I stopped and looked behind at Sarah. "Why did you stop like that?" she snapped at me. "I could've fallen."

"Did you call the police?" I asked her, standing my ground.

"No!" She made to push past me, but I hurried ahead.

We all rushed into the tunnel just as the wind picked up force again. Once more, I found going down harder work than going up, probably because it was hard to keep my footing. It would be a long way to fall, and there were no guide rails. I tensed every time I heard a movement behind me, wondering if someone would push me. Nevertheless, the tunnel did wind around and level out for short distances regularly, so anyone who was pushed would be able to break their fall easily enough. I kept a close eye on Owen and made sure he stayed in front of me.

I made a mental note to take up some exercise and to stop eating so many cupcakes. It seemed that we had been gone for a very long time, but that was probably because of my lack of fitness. Vanessa and Sarah, to the contrary, looked like they spent a lot of time in the gym.

My calves were aching by the time I reached the flat tunnel. Once again, the wind was violent between the two tunnels and once more I was thoroughly soaked. Blisters were forming on my heels from walking all the way in soaking wet shoes. On the bright side, it had all been worth it because I had got the message to Alder telling him of my predicament. The thought warmed me right through.

As I sprinted for the entrance of the flat tunnel, I noticed there was only one axe in the chopping block. Perhaps I had only imagined two before. I ran faster as the hairs on the back of my neck stood up.

I ran blindly into the tunnel and bumped into Owen, sending him stumbling forward. "Oh my gosh, I'm so sorry!" I said.

He nodded and moved forward. No doubt he hadn't heard what I said, because we were too close to the entrance and the wind was deafening. Thunder had started again and the ground shook with every thunder clap. I was glad there had been no lightning when we were at the top of the hill.

We reached the tunnel door which Owen pulled open, and we walked into his office. The light hurt my eyes and I blinked rapidly. Vanessa was right behind me, and she was out of breath. I wondered why, because that was the first time I had seen her puffing. "Where's Sarah?" Owen said.

Vanessa looked behind her. "I thought she was right behind me."

Owen called out, but there was no response. "Come on, all three of us will have to go back and look for her. Stay close, mind you."

Don't ask me how, but I just knew something was terribly wrong. I didn't want to go back into the tunnel, but I knew I had no choice. I stayed close to Owen and Vanessa as we made our way back along the tunnel.

The sense of dread increased with every step.

We reached the end of the tunnel and stopped. "We couldn't have passed her," Owen said. "The tunnel isn't wide enough."

"Something's happened to her," I said with certainty. No one disagreed with me.

Owen turned to Vanessa. "When did you last see her?"

Vanessa was shaking. "Um, it must've been when we ran out of the tunnel. I was ahead of her and the wind was so strong that I just sprinted as fast as I could. I was right behind you guys." She appeared to be on the verge of tears.

"The axe was missing!" I said, suddenly remembering. "On the way out, I saw two axes, and on the way back, I only saw one. I thought I must've imagined it the first time, but now..." My voice trailed away.

We hurried back down the tunnel, shining our flashlights on every nook and cranny. When we reached the end of the tunnel, instead of sprinting for the next tunnel, we all stepped forward, shielding our faces from the wind and scanning the area.

Owen was the first to speak. "Ladies, turn around. Don't look."

I ignored his request and looked past him, and over by a fallen tree, I could see Sarah. The axe was impaled in her head.

It was all so surreal. I tried to speak, but no words would come out. Vanessa must be the killer. If no one else was on the island, then it had to be Vanessa. Owen had been in front of me the whole time. That is, unless Vanessa and Owen were in it together.

The blood drained from my face as I turned to look at the chopping block. The axe was still there. I could have cried with relief.

I felt as if I were going to faint, but now was not the time and place to sit down and put my head between my legs, not with a murderer likely watching me right now. If it wasn't Vanessa, then it had to be someone else on the island, somebody that no one else knew was there. And the others had said that there was no one else on the island.

I looked at Vanessa to see if she had any blood splatters on her, but the rain would have washed them away. Owen must have been thinking the same thing. "Vanessa, why is there mud all down the front of your clothes?"

"I was running so fast that I tripped and fell face forward in the tunnel," she said. Her voice was trembling and she looked ashen, but I supposed that someone who had murdered more than once would be a good actor. She had obviously put mud on her clothes to hide any blood splatters that hadn't washed away in the rain.

Owen's face was green and he looked as though he was about to be sick. "There's nothing we can do for Sarah now. Let's go back and tell the others what's happened. The three of us need to stick together." He shot me a significant look as he said it, and I assumed he was trying to give me the hint that Vanessa was the killer. I had already figured that out for myself. It was screamingly obvious, and I wondered why it hadn't occurred to Vanessa that we would know it was her.

The three of us hurried back down the tunnel, and I was sure to keep a close eye on Vanessa.

I had another horrible thought. What if someone, or even all of the others, had been murdered? It had already occurred to me that there could be more than one murderer. I was sick to my stomach.

After we reached the office, we wasted no time hurrying back to the dining room. I was at once relieved to see that Abby and Michael were sitting there, calm and well.

"Where's Sarah?" Michael asked, when the three of us burst into the room, soaking wet and frantic.

Owen did not mince words. "She's been

murdered with an axe," he said grimly. "It's only just happened."

Mandy appeared at the kitchen door with a coffee pot. "What?" she screeched.

Lisa, towel-drying her hair, hurried into the room. "What's happened?"

Everyone gathered around us, all speaking at once, all asking questions.

Owen held up a hand for silence. "We made it to the top of the hill, and you'll be pleased to know I was able to speak to the police, although the service was intermittent at best. They're going to come as soon as the storm breaks. Amelia and I were coming back along the second tunnel, and we thought Vanessa and Sarah were right behind us. When we reached the office, we realised that Sarah wasn't there. Vanessa said she had last seen her at the second tunnel, so we all went back, and we found Sarah. She had been killed with an axe. Michael and I will have to go back for her, and put her in the cool room with the others."

There was a collective gasp, and everyone turned to Vanessa. I watched as it dawned on her. She clutched her throat. "It wasn't me! I tell you, there must be someone else on the island. It wasn't me!"

"It wasn't me, and it wasn't Amelia," Owen said evenly. "The two of us were close together the whole time, and Vanessa was the only one lagging behind."

Vanessa was struck silent, her jaw working up and down. I wondered how she would try to get out of this one. I supposed she had seen the two axes on the way up the hill, and had moved one ready for the return journey. No doubt she hadn't had time to think it through and had simply seized her opportunity.

"It wasn't me, I tell you!" she said again, her voice filled with panic. "I was right behind Owen and Amelia in the tunnel. I hadn't realised Sarah had fallen back. I'm telling you, there's someone else on the island!"

"You poor thing," Mandy said, ignoring Vanessa and patting me on the shoulder. "You're drenched. I'll get you and Owen some fresh coffee. This coffee pot's cold for some reason." She hurried back to the kitchen.

"What will we do with Vanessa?" Michael addressed the question to Owen.

"There's a storeroom out back," Owen said. "It doesn't have windows and we can lock the door. It's part of the original building—it was once a servant's room. It has a tiny bathroom now and even a small opening at the top of the door. It'll make an ideal prison cell."

Vanessa clutched at her throat and backed away. "You can't lock me up! It wasn't me!"

Just then, a loud scream erupted from the kitchen.

CHAPTER 8

*M*andy ran out, her eyes wide and her arms outstretched. She was as white as a ghost, and unable to speak.

"Stay here, all of you," Michael called over his shoulder, "Keep an eye on her." Owen ran after him to the kitchen.

They returned shortly after with the pool boy. I would recognise those abs anywhere.

Michael pushed him into a chair. "What are you doing here, Bazza?"

Bazza ran his hand through his dreadlocks. "What's all the fuss? Why the rough treatment, man?"

"You were supposed to have left the island yesterday," Owen said angrily. "Explain yourself!"

Bazza leaned back. "What's the problem? I had a migraine so I went to bed, and when I woke up, I'd missed the boat. I was sick from the migraine, so I slept all night until this morning. I'm off duty, anyway, so why does anyone care what I do? What's going on?"

"Why are you soaking wet? Where's your shirt?" Michael asked him.

"Duh! I've just had a shower."

"Why are your shorts soaking wet, then?" Michael said.

Bazza shrugged and looked unconcerned. "I didn't want to bother drying myself too much because I was starving. I was in a hurry to get some food. What's wrong with that? It's not against the law, is it?" He laughed at his own joke and then studied his thumbnail.

"But *murder* is against the law," Michael said.

Bazza's expression changed. "Are you for real?"

"Two of our guests, Benedict Fletcher and Laura Lindsey, were stabbed to death last night, and Sarah Stafford was murdered only minutes ago, outside the tunnel with an axe. But you already knew that, didn't you!" Michael added.

Bazza shook his head. "You're kidding, right?"

When no one spoke, he jumped to his feet and pushed the chair back. "Murder? Here?"

Michael shoved him back into the chair. "Stay right where you are, and don't make any sudden moves."

Bazza looked wildly around him. He shot from his chair and made to run away, but he didn't get far. Michael and Owen grabbed him. He struggled wildly at first, but stopped when he saw it was no use. "Seriously, man, I didn't do it. It wasn't me."

"Let's put him in that room we talked about earlier," Owen said to Michael.

"It wasn't me," Bazza said again.

Owen and Michael escorted him out of the room, and all the while he was protesting his innocence.

I didn't know what to believe. Bazza was soaking wet and shirtless. At this point it seemed to come down to either him or Vanessa, but I couldn't believe either of them did it. Still, I had to remind myself that *someone* was the murderer. Both Bazza and Vanessa had the opportunity, and for all I knew, one of the others in the room could have slipped out somehow and murdered Sarah. I couldn't see how, but I had to admit that it was a possibility. Lisa had been wet and was drying her hair. And whoever it was, was acting normal. They weren't going to do anything to give themselves away and so I had to stay on full alert.

I was relieved that the police knew what was happening and were coming, and that Alder knew. He would have told the others by now and they were no doubt doing spells for my protection. I also had done spells for my protection, but I was still worried. Who wouldn't be?

Yet what motive could the murderer or murderers possibly have? I had no idea. What connection was there between Benedict, Laura, and Sarah? If Benedict was the target, then Laura simply could have been there at the wrong time, and the same could be said for Benedict if Laura had been the target. Yet what did either of them have to do with Sarah? I remembered that Sarah was a journalist. Benedict was a famous food critic, and he had said he had a scoop for her, so there was a connection right there. It might not have anything to do with the murder, but it was a plausible strand of evidence for a possible motive.

There was also the possibility that one person was the target, and the other two had been murdered to cover up that fact, to throw the police off the track.

I wondered if anyone else could be on the island, someone undetected, but I thought it unlikely. The cooking school resort was the only building on the island, and the wind had been furious. I supposed there was the possibility that someone had been hiding in the tunnels, and had only left their cover when they heard us coming. Yet for what purpose? *Obviously to murder someone*, I thought.

I sat on a chair and rubbed my tense neck. I wondered what the dripping sound was, and then realised I was still soaking wet and needed a hot shower. There was no way I was going to walk to my room alone, and I didn't want just one person to accompany me there. Everyone was standing around looking at each other. I spoke up. "Would you all walk me to my room, please? I'm soaking wet and I don't want to go alone."

"You're safe now that the murderer's been locked up," Mandy said.

"But what makes you think he's the murderer?" Lisa said. "We don't know for sure. It's just as likely to be one of us. I, for one, won't be taking any chances. It had to be Vanessa—who else had the opportunity to murder Sarah?"

"Someone could have sneaked out and done

it," Abby said. "Some of us took bathroom breaks and you can't see the bathroom door from here. Lisa, you took a long shower break, didn't you? And Mandy, you were an awfully long time making coffee. The first tunnel isn't very long. Anyone could've sneaked out there and waited for Sarah."

"I'm afraid your shower will have to wait, Amelia." I swung around at Owen's voice. I hadn't even seen Owen and Michael return. "We'll need to bag Vanessa's shirt as evidence."

Vanessa jumped to her feet. "Over my dead body!"

I couldn't believe she had just said that. She continued to screech, clutching her hands over her chest. "You're not having my shirt!"

"Yes, we are." Michael took a step towards her, and she backed up against the dining table. "Abby and Amelia will escort you to your room, and wait until you change." He walked over to Abby and handed her a large plastic bag. "Abby, have Vanessa put the shirt in there—make sure you don't touch it. Then tie a knot in the bag tightly and bring it back to me. We'll put it in the cool room with the bodies."

Vanessa stomped her foot. "Keep away from me!"

"You have two choices, Vanessa," Michael said firmly. "We either lock you in a room until the police come, or you can stay out here with the rest of us on the condition that you give us your shirt."

Vanessa's cheeks puffed up like those of a two-year-old child about to have a tantrum. She appeared to be thinking it over. "Fine!" she snapped. "I'm doing this under protest. And I'm going to make a written complaint to..." She appeared to be trying to figure out to whom she could make the complaint, and failed. "I *am* going to make a complaint!"

Owen nodded to Abby. "Come on, Amelia. The two of you take Vanessa to her room and make sure you get her shirt. Make sure she doesn't wash it first. She has to take it straight off and put it in the bag. Don't take your eyes off her. Don't take too long, because Michael and I have to go and get, um, the body and put it in the cool room with the others." His face was ashen.

Abby and I trailed behind a furious Vanessa. I wondered if she would slam the door on our faces before we got into her room, but Abby must have been anticipating that as well, because she barged straight in as soon as Vanessa unlocked the door.

"I'm just going to the bathroom to take off my

shirt, and you two can wait out here," Vanessa said imperiously.

Abby shook her head. "No, we have to watch you at all times."

"Why?" Vanessa said angrily. "What do you think I'm going to do?"

"That was the deal," Abby said. "Either give us your shirt now, in this room, or Owen and Michael will lock you up."

I wondered how Abby was managing to stay so calm.

"Fine!" Vanessa stormed over to the dresser and pulled out another shirt. "Can I ask you to have the common decency to shut your eyes? I'll stand right here and you'll hear if I move. I don't like people looking at me."

Abby and I exchanged glances, and Abby nodded slightly. "All right then, but make it fast. Owen and Michael are waiting." She handed her the plastic bag.

Vanessa snatched it and turned her back to us.

Abby shut her eyes, and I did, too. Moments later, I heard a rustling sound, and I assumed that Abby was pushing the shirt into the bag. Right at that moment, there was a clap of thunder. I instinctively opened my eyes. There was a mirror to the side of the wall, and in it I saw Vanessa clearly. She had a nasty scar on her chest. For a moment, I had a rare pang of sympathy for her. I immediately shut my eyes again.

"Finished! Are you happy now?"

I opened my eyes and saw Abby had already opened hers. Vanessa viciously thrust the bag at her. "And now I'd like to have a shower, *in private*. If you ladies don't want to watch, would you be *so kind* as to wait out here for me. And Amelia, remove yourself from my bed. You're dripping all over it."

I moved to stand near the door where I was dripping puddles of water only on the tiles. Despite the humidity, I was beginning to shiver, and I hoped her shower would be fast.

It was not to be. Vanessa's shower was no doubt the longest shower in the history of the earth, and I was sure it was just to spite me.

When she finally emerged, I was shaking and hungry. "Come along, Amelia," Abby said. "We'll take you to your room. You're shivering."

When we reached my door, I asked them to wait while I checked the rooms. I felt a little silly doing so, but I wanted to be careful. When I saw the room was clear, I thanked them and locked the door.

I stood under the shower for ages, thankful for the hot water. I was stressed to the max. This was an absolute nightmare. I wanted to wash away the memory of seeing Sarah, and Benedict and Laura for that matter. The hot water revived me somewhat, and the heat on my neck made me realise just how tense my muscles had been. The water stung my blisters, but that was the least of my worries. My calves were still aching, but I was too tense to enjoy a long hot bath. There were numerous suspects, yet no clear motive. My goal was to remain alive until the police arrived, and I would have a far better chance of doing so if I knew the identity of the murderer.

After I towelled myself dry and dressed, I rubbed some cream on my heels. The blisters were raw and peeling, so I decided to stay barefoot. That's when it dawned on me. How was I going to get out of my room? I felt so silly. I should have asked the others to return in fifteen minutes. Now I would either have to stay in my room, or go back to the dining room where I assumed the others were still gathered.

I rested my ear against the door, and heard no

one. My heart was beating out of my chest and my breathing was rapid and shallow. I wiped my palms on my jeans and looked around the room for something to use as a weapon. I came up empty.

I forced myself to think logically. The others were hardly going to let someone wander off alone, so it was unlikely that the murderer would be able to get away from the group to harm me. However, the murderer might be someone outside the building, someone unknown. Yet if that were the case, surely such a person would not risk exposure by walking through the house.

I sat back on the bed, my head in my hands. This was all too much. I was going around in circles and not coming to any conclusion. If I stayed in my room, I would go mad, not to mention starve. I had to get back out to the dining room. My stomach growling loudly made the decision for me.

I decided I would just have to make a break for it. I crept once more to the door and listened. Again there was no sound. I decided to sneak along the corridor, and if I saw anyone coming, I would run. I was a fast runner, and I would be even faster if there was a murderer right behind me.

I gingerly opened the door with the ball of my foot pressed against it in case someone tried to burst into the room. I opened it a little wider and peeped out. Not a sign of anyone. I stepped into the corridor and shut the door behind me as quietly as I could, while looking around me. So far, so good.

I tiptoed down the corridor stealthily, which was easy, given the fact my feet were bare. To my great relief, I encountered no one. I slowed when I approached the entrance to the kitchen, listening for footsteps.

There were muffled noises coming from the kitchen. It didn't sound like anyone preparing food, and I couldn't hear anyone talking.

I waited, but the noises continued. I took a deep breath and willed myself to look. I wasn't prepared for what I saw.

CHAPTER 9

*M*ichael and Abby were kissing passionately.

I averted my eyes and ducked back into the corridor. I had no idea if they had seen me, but I had no option except to move forward. I reached the dining room without further incident. I almost staggered with relief when I saw everyone sitting there alive and well.

"Amelia, I was just about to go back for you," Mandy said. "Not alone, of course. We were all going to go for you."

I thanked her.

"We'll all have to stay together from now on," Owen said. He turned to the kitchen. "I hope Abby and Michael are okay. I'd better go check."

I didn't know whether to say anything to stop him walking in on them, but I was saved from having to make the decision. The two of them walked out carrying trays of coffee and cups, looking as if butter wouldn't melt in their mouths.

Owen stood up. "There's something I need to say. This has all been a big shock to me, we're all like a little family here." He cleared his throat and flushed beet red. "This has to be said. I know we locked up Bazza, but I'm not convinced Bazza is the murderer." Everyone murmured, and Owen held up his hand. "I know you all must be thinking the same thing, or why else would none of us go anywhere alone?"

Lisa agreed. "I'm sure it's not Bazza."

"Better to be safe than sorry," Abby said. "It's not as if he's faced a court of law—yet. We took him on earlier this year at the recommendation of the last pool boy who left in a hurry. We really don't know much about him."

"We really don't know anything about anyone here," Lisa pointed out. "Mandy and I have been coming here for some time, and nothing like this has ever happened before. I've always found Bazza to be a nice, helpful man. I'm sure it wasn't him." She looked around nervously as she spoke.

"Amelia and I were together in the tunnel when Sarah was murdered," Owen said. "So that rules both of us out, and I think it's fair to say that whoever killed Sarah also killed Benedict and Laura."

Vanessa set down her coffee with a thud. "True, but that doesn't rule out there being two murderers. There could be two people in it together."

Everyone looked around the table with fear in their eyes.

"It *is* certainly possible that two people are in it together," Michael said. "But for all we know, Bazza has a criminal record. The police could be looking for him at this very moment. He's only been here a short time, so he could be fleeing from anything. Maybe he left a trail of murders behind him on the mainland."

Abby gently rocked her chair and twirled her coffee cup around several times. Everyone's attention turned to her. "Here's one way to put this to rest. We need to go back up the hill and tell the police about Bazza, if that's even his real name. If they say he *is* wanted for murder, then we can all rest easy, since he's locked up with no hope of escape. Then we won't all be suspecting each other and jumping at every sound."

Everyone agreed, but I had my doubts. Was that just a ploy to get everyone up the hill to pick off one more victim? I remembered the words of Mulder on *The X-Files*, "Trust no one."

Owen sat down, and spoke before anyone else had the opportunity. "Now we all know that we can't leave the island until the storm clears and the police come, and the circumstances are far from pleasant. Nonetheless, I think we should continue the cooking school."

Everyone erupted into chatter. Lisa was the first to speak. "Isn't that a little disrespectful? Of the dead, I mean."

Owen shook his head. "It could be two to three days, possibly more, possibly less—who knows?— before the police can get here. What are we all going to do during that time? No one can swim, no one can walk along the beach, not in the storm. We could all sit here and read, and go crazy trying to think who the perpetrator or perpetrators could be, or we can continue with the cooking school. That will give us something to focus on."

I could see everyone was coming around to the idea, and that made me somewhat concerned.

Once they sampled my cooking, they would no doubt be convinced I was the murderer, and I would spend the next few days locked in a small room. That reminded me of Marcel de Vries, the chef who had already fallen victim to my baking. "Owen, are you sure the French chef left on the boat?" I asked him. "I mean, did you see him leave and sail away?"

Owen seemed taken aback. "Why, yes."

I pressed the matter. "Did you actually see him leave, or could he have got off the boat when you walked away?"

Owen rubbed his chin. "I put him on the boat and then I left. I saw the boat leave, but I suppose it's always possible he did get off, hypothetically speaking. I'm sure he didn't, though. I mean, what reason would he have to get off the boat?"

I shrugged. "What reason would *anyone* have to murder Benedict, Laura, and Sarah?"

"I think Amelia's right," Lisa chimed in. "Perhaps he was faking his teeth falling out. Maybe it was so we'd all think he'd left the island, and he could sneak off the boat and double back and murder everyone."

"Amelia would be the first person he'd murder

if that was the case," Vanessa said smugly, shooting me a look of pure spite.

"No, that's just it!" Lisa exclaimed. "I just said he was faking his teeth. I mean, how can anyone lose their teeth just from biting a chocolate chip cookie?"

"Trust me, he wasn't faking it," I said sadly.

"Let's not worry about Marcel de Vries for now," Owen continued. "We'll all go stir crazy sitting around here staring at the four walls. Haven't you heard of cabin fever? Or the expression *Going Troppo?* Those expressions refer to people who are locked up like we are. We might as well continue the cooking lessons. What else can we do? Needless to say, Abby and I will refund you the costs of your stay here, so I'm not speaking for financial reasons. I just think we need to do something to occupy ourselves." He paused to look at everyone in turn. "And then there's the problem of the meals. The meals are made by all the students, with our help. If we are all going to prepare the food, as planned, then we might as well continue with the lessons."

"I do think it's a good idea," Vanessa said. "I'm awfully bored already."

She didn't appear to see anything wrong with

what she had said. I found it rather disrespectful to the victims, but then again, I hadn't found Vanessa to be a pleasant type of person.

Owen looked satisfied. "All right then, since everyone's in agreement, we'll carry on with our cooking lesson schedule as originally intended. And then, after the cooking lesson and lunch, we'll decide who will go up the hill this time."

"Do you think there really could be someone else on the island?" Mandy asked. "If not the chef, then someone else?"

Michael joined the conversation. "It's highly unlikely, but of course, anything's possible. All we can do is keep ourselves safe until the police come. If we *do* find out that Bazza is wanted for murder or some other terrible crime, then we can stop suspecting each other. Right now, I suggest we prepare lunch. Let's all go to the teaching kitchen."

With a heavy heart I walked with the others to the teaching kitchen. I wondered what disaster I would have to prepare for lunch. I didn't have long to wait. Abby immediately distributed a laminated sheet to everyone. "Here's your recipe. We're going to make something incredibly simple for our first lunch: Mexican beans with Avocado Salsa. What could be more simple?"

Only with difficulty did I remain silent. Owen walked along, distributing the ingredients to everybody.

Abby gestured to the steel work benches. "Each of you take your place at a countertop. We will be making this easy meal in a pressure cooker. It's foolproof."

"That's what you think," I muttered.

"Amelia, did you say something?"

"No," I lied. I nervously eyed the beans.

"Rinse the pinto beans and remove any tiny stones from them," Abby instructed. She demonstrated as she spoke.

At least that was something I could do well. I rinsed the dried pinto beans and picked through them, looking for any foreign matter. I probably spent too long rinsing my beans, because I looked around and saw others were fastening their lids. I quickly consulted the recipe, and added the required cups of water and the tablespoon of extra virgin olive oil. I poured them all into the high pressure cooker and then shut the lid. I set the pressure cooker to high pressure. What a relief! It had all gone far better than I thought it would.

Now I saw that everyone was chopping up vegetables. The recipe told me to chop up the bell peppers and the onion. I wondered at the wisdom of giving large sharp knives to possible murderers, but I supposed there was no option.

Now the part I was dreading. It said to heat a teaspoon of oil in a large frying pan and sauté the vegetables for three to five minutes. I was terrified. Most of my baking accidents were something to do with flames.

I very cautiously heated the oil, having put in a little less than the recipe required, and very carefully put in the vegetables. I kept an eye on the flame, but so far all was going according to plan, much to my surprise. I reluctantly dragged my gaze from the flames to look at the recipe and saw that I had to add oregano, ground cumin, and minced garlic, and then cook a further two minutes.

It was with enormous relief that I turned off the gas and removed the frying pan from the heat. One thing was for sure, my cooking was definitely improving. The recipe then required that I remove the beans and drain them, but not rinse them. I did that, feeling a sense of achievement. I then placed the beans back into the pressure cooker with the sautéed mixture, along with three cups of vegetable broth. This time, I had to cook the mixture for six minutes at high pressure. I turned the pressure cooker to high, and checked my watch. What a relief! I was all almost done. Now I just had to make the salsa, but that did not include any baking.

I looked up at Abby, and she was nodding at me approvingly. I diced the avocados into small pieces and put them in a glass bowl, and then poured on some lime juice. I paused to see what everyone else was doing. It seemed I had caught up to them, because they were all dicing avocados as well.

"Well done, everyone," Owen said. "Now we just have to wait for the beans to cook, and then we'll season them to taste with freshly ground sea salt and black pepper. We will serve them hot with the salsa in the dining room. I'm sure everyone will enjoy a hearty meal." He was about to say more, when there was an almighty explosion.

At first I thought someone had thrown a hand grenade into the room and was firing bullets at us. We all dived under our benches.

I peered out from my place of safety, terror-stricken. Finally, the assault stopped and I gingerly crawled out.

"It's safe to stand up now." Abby sounded

angry rather than scared. I wondered why there was an edge to her voice.

"But someone's trying to shoot at us," Lisa said.

"No, it was just an accident," Abby said, with the same edge to her voice.

I stood up, as did the others, and saw that Abby was pointing to the ceiling. I followed her gaze. There was a pressure cooker lid wedged in the ceiling above me.

I looked back at the others. They had beans stuck to various parts of their body. Owen had a bean wedged in his ear, and a bean was stuck on the middle of Michael's forehead. Abby had a row of beans in the formation of a tiara stuck to her hair. I considered pointing this out to her, and then thought maybe I should not.

"Let this be a lesson to you all to make *very* sure the pressure cooker lid is secured firmly," Abby said tersely.

CHAPTER 10

*a*fter lunch—and thankfully people had shared their beans with me—there was a lively discussion as to who should go back up the hill. Once again, nobody had any objections to me going, no doubt thanks to my spell to ensure that would happen.

"I think I should go," Owen said, "and Michael should stay with the remaining people."

Abby crossed the room to look out the shutters. "I want to stay."

"I'll stay with Abby," Mandy said.

"I'm not going," Vanessa screeched. "And what if the food's poisoned? We'll all die if we eat it, or starve if we don't."

A hush fell over the room. That idea had not

occurred to me, nor to anyone else, judging by the looks on their faces. It was a strange change of subject, but I thought it a valid point.

"I know you're the murderer," Lisa piped up. She stood up and pointed at Vanessa, who simply rolled her eyes.

"And what makes you think that, Sherlock?" Vanessa asked.

"It's either you or Bazza, and I know it isn't him. I can't think of anyone else."

I silently agreed with Lisa. If it wasn't the pool boy, then Vanessa was the next likely suspect. I would have locked her up with him, but I didn't know whether that was just because I didn't like her.

Vanessa leaped from her seat, and Michael hurried to separate the two women. She pursed her lips. "I'm not going up the hill again!"

After Vanessa declared she was staying, Mandy and Abby said they wanted to go up the hill. I wondered if that was because they secretly thought Vanessa might have had a hand in Sarah's murder.

"I'm getting a headache," Lisa said, rapidly standing up and rubbing her forehead. "I can't go, after all."

"It's settled, then," Vanessa said. "Lisa and I will stay."

I saw Owen and Michael exchange glances. "I have to go to my room," Lisa added. "I feel really sick. I think it's a stress headache."

"Michael and I will take you to your room," Owen said. "Make sure you lock your door, and don't open it to anyone. I mean *anyone*. When we come back, we'll knock on your door. Make sure you hear two voices before you open the door. Bazza's locked in the room, so don't go near him. Michael and I will check on Bazza to make sure he *is* still safely in his makeshift prison cell."

We were all quiet while Michael and Owen were gone. I wondered if Vanessa really would insist on staying on her own. That would be foolhardy, to say the least.

"I was hoping the storm would be on its way out by now," Owen said upon his return, "but it looks as though that's not the case. Now, we have to settle the matter of who stays and who goes. Will anyone stay behind with Vanessa? We need two people. Lisa will be in her room, so she doesn't count."

His remark was met with dead silence. There were no volunteers. "Vanessa, you'll have to come with us," Owen said, "unless you want to stay locked in your room."

Vanessa left her chair, her face red and her eyes narrowed into slits. "All right then, but I'll have you know, I'm coming under protest!" She pushed past Owen and stormed out of the room.

Once again, I wasn't keen to go up the hill, but I would do anything to get a chance to speak to Alder, or even send him a message. And like the last time, I had already written a text and so all I had to do was send it as soon as I had service. Hopefully, there would again be reception up the top of the hill. I couldn't shake off the reminder that Sarah had been murdered on my last venture up the hill, so I hoped nothing would happen this time, especially not to me. I did suspect Vanessa, so I was disappointed that she was not staying behind. I intended to stick like glue to Owen, because my suspicions had been right—Sarah and Vanessa had been the two to bring up the rear, and look what had happened to Sarah! It's always the ones who bring up the rear who get killed.

I wasn't as scared entering the tunnel as I had been the first time. After all, I was now familiar with the tunnels, but Mandy was none too thrilled, judging by her comments. I had my phone in my pocket in case the flashlight batteries failed, and I had charged my phone.

The first thing I noticed was the smell and the cold. The interior of the building itself was warm, but the tunnel had a kind of damp coolness to it. It was as if the walls exuded moisture. It was not a comforting feeling, rather one of some type of hidden threat. And in fact, I supposed that danger did indeed lurk around every corner.

Mandy clung to my arm. "It's not too bad," I said in an attempt to reassure her. "This tunnel doesn't go for too long, and then we come out into the jungle. Well, it's not exactly a jungle, but we come out of this tunnel into it, and it's like tropical undergrowth and stuff." I knew I was not making much sense, but I continued regardless. "Then we have to sprint to the next tunnel because it's horribly windy. Then we go uphill and there are lots of stairs, but it's not as bad as you think, because the tunnel is wide and not at all scary." *If you don't reckon on the axe wielding murderers*, I added silently.

When we reached the end of the tunnel, I saw that one axe was firmly still in the chopping block. The wind wasn't as violent now, but I clung to every tree I passed so it didn't blow me over.

Thunder was rapidly approaching, and the air pressure was building. It was as if the whole environment was on an adrenaline rush.

We all sprinted after Owen across the gap between the tunnels. Mandy did her best to stick closely to Owen, and I did my best to shoulder her out of the way without being too obvious about it. Lightning flashed as I ran between the tunnels, my heels painful and bleeding.

Vanessa complained at length for the entire second tunnel, saying she was short of breath and needed to sit down. I doubted she would sit in the dirt, and when Michael finally called her bluff and said we should all stop while she rested, she merely leaned against the wall. I was tempted to suggest leaving her there until our return.

My calves were burning by the time I reached the top of the stairs, but that was nothing compared to the pain in my heels. Again, I would have much rather stayed in the safety of the building, but I figured I had to be the safest person on the island, given my own protection spells and those of my friends. And as before, there was no way I would miss an opportunity to speak with Alder.

I was relieved when we finally left the tunnel

and climbed the rocky embankment to the top of the hill. It was still more sheltered than the place between the tunnels. I thought that strange as it was on the top of the hill, but I supposed the outcrop of rocks provided some shelter. I fell into the same pattern as before, pressing 'send' continually until the message sent. This time, there was a message from Alder, telling me that he and the others were doing spells for my protection. He asked me to call him as soon as I could.

I was able to get through on the third call. "Amelia! Are you all right? What's happened?"

"I've texted you all the details. There's been another murder, Alder! They suspect the pool boy, Bazza Aston. Would you see if you could find out anything about him? Alder, I'm really scared."

"Amelia..." With that, the connection dropped out.

CHAPTER 11

I looked up to see Mandy speaking, and the others furiously tapping their phones. Owen, too, was speaking, so I tried to call Alder back. I expected I had a different mobile phone carrier to Owen and Mandy. Obviously, I hadn't picked a good one.

I typed another message and tried to send it. Again, I sat with my back to the rock and watched the others. Abby and Michael presently joined me.

The thunder was progressing from low rumbles to loud cracks. I counted the intervals between the lightning and the thunder, and soon the thunder was upon us. There was a simultaneous crack of thunder and flash of lightning. I jumped as the lightning struck a tree on the verge of the clearing.

Electricity reverberated through my body as the ground trembled. The tree fell away from our group, but it nonetheless gave me quite a fright. Mandy and Vanessa were astonished, but Owen had the presence of mind to take them by the arms and escort them to my somewhat sheltered position at speed. "Quick everyone, back into the tunnel as fast as you can. I'll tell you what the police said once we're back undercover."

We ran to the tunnel entrance and stumbled inside. I pressed my back to the wall and kept an eye on the entrance. I shone my flashlight down into the tunnel to make sure no one was waiting there for us.

We were all breathing rapidly, and Owen, I assume, waited until we were all calmer before speaking. "I got through to the police again. They said they had done background checks on all the guests, and didn't find anything unusual. I told them all about poor Sarah's murder, and also that Bazza was still on the island."

"Did they do a background check on him?" Mandy asked.

Owen shook his head, or so I assumed in the dim lighting at the entrance to the tunnel. We were far enough inside that the wind didn't penetrate it and lash us, but not so far that we were enveloped in total darkness. "No," Owen said. "I didn't know that Bazza was still on the island when Benedict and Laura were killed." With that, he headed into the tunnel, with me right behind him.

Tears were streaming down my face at the pain in my heels. The blisters were red raw and bleeding, and to say they hurt was an understatement. I did consider taking off my shoes, but that would mean I would lag behind, and goodness knows what was on the tunnel floor. I certainly couldn't afford to gash my feet, though the blisters were horribly painful. Every step was agony, but the alternative would have been far worse.

It wasn't long before I was overtaken, and I struggled to keep up with the others. Even if it weren't for the bad blisters on my feet, the others were keeping up an incredible pace. I assumed they were as worried as I was about being out in the storm, potentially with a murderer, no less. I called out to them, but the group quickly disappeared into the darkness ahead of me.

I hobbled forward as quickly as I possibly could, trying my best to ignore the severe pain shooting through my feet. I considered taking off my shoes again, but decided that the pain was only temporary. I didn't want to gash my feet on something rusty—who knew what was lying on the tunnel floors.

Alone in the tunnel, the darkness felt more oppressive than ever. I was thankful for my flashlight, but I couldn't shake the awful feeling of someone, or something, standing behind me. I spun around several times to shine my light back through the tunnel, but each time there was nothing, and it was slowing me down. I had to speed up if I wanted any chance of catching the others.

Finally, I arrived at the exit of the second tunnel. I had to make it across the clearing, then there was just the other tunnel and I'd be free. I'd hoped that the others would be waiting at the entrance of that tunnel for me, but it was too dark to see inside.

I looked out across the clearing and gulped nervously. The wind still wasn't nearly as bad as it had been during our first expedition to the hill, but knowing that Sarah had been murdered here was almost more than I could bear. It did, however, provide plenty of motivation to ignore the stinging pain of my blisters as I sprinted across the clearing and into the next tunnel.

As soon as I was inside, I fell backwards and sat down with a thud, exhausted and terrified. There was still no sign of the group, though of course they had probably made it back inside by now. I shone my flashlight into the tunnel and sighed deeply when I realised I would have to make the entire trip back alone.

I gingerly stood to my feet, propping myself against the wall for support. I slowly began the walk back through the tunnel, hoping that my feeling of nervousness would pass before long, though I doubted it very much.

After a few steps, that same feeling of being watched returned. I shuddered and spun around, partially hoping I'd catch someone looking at me, but simultaneously very much hoping I wouldn't.

Through the entrance I had just come from, I briefly saw someone dart past the clearing. I barely had a glimpse of whoever it was, but it was enough to make me sprint the rest of the way back, regardless of the pain in my feet. It couldn't have been any of the group, since they had been with me most of the way and I would have noticed if someone had doubled back. If it was anyone else, I couldn't imagine that they had good intentions.

About a minute into my record-setting run back down the tunnel, I was temporarily blinded by several bright lights.

"Amelia!" Owen's voice sounded out as he ran towards me. I fell to the ground in a heap, barely managing to hold back hot tears. The tears were partly from fear and adrenaline, but mostly from pain. I couldn't wait to take those stupid shoes off. "Are you all right? What happened?"

"There's someone else out here," I managed to say, shining my light back through the tunnel. There was nothing but bricks and dirt.

"Are you sure? What happened?" Owen asked, kneeling beside me and putting his hands on my shoulders.

"My blisters slowed me down, so I fell behind," I explained, resisting the urge to chew them out for not coming back to check on me, or at least waiting a little while. "Just after I ran through the clearing, I looked back and saw a person."

"Who was it?" Mandy asked, clearly terrified.

"I don't know," I sighed. "I barely saw them, and I didn't exactly want to stick around."

"It was probably just a large bird of some

kind," Owen said dismissively. "We get them around here from time to time. That, combined with the stress of everything and your pain, probably made you assume the worst."

I was a bit annoyed at Owen's condescending attitude, but I had to admit that he had a point. Did I really know that it had been a person? Could it have been something else? I thought back to the moment, trying my best to remember. The figure had been moving quickly, but I was sure it was human. I looked up at the group.

"It was definitely a person," I said with a nod. "I just can't say for sure who it was. I don't even know their gender."

"But who else could it be?" Michael asked. "We're the only ones on the island, aren't we?"

The question caused a wave of uneasiness to shoot through me. After all, we had always thought we were alone on the island, but then Bazza had shown up. Anybody else could have skipped off the boat onto the island, or even come here by some other means entirely.

CHAPTER 12

"*L*et's go and see how Lisa is," Owen said as soon as we emerged from the tunnel into the safety of the office. I knew he really meant to say to see if Lisa was still alive, and that's what I had been thinking, too. I had a lump in my throat as we all followed Owen down the corridor to Lisa's room. Owen and Abby spoke at once and asked her to unlock the door. She did presently, and looked none the worse for wear.

"How are you feeling now?" Abby asked her.

"Fine, thank you. I only woke up a few minutes ago. Is everyone all right? How did it go?"

"I'll tell you when we get to the dining room," Owen said. "Meanwhile, Michael and I will go check on Bazza."

I went with the other women to the dining room, but Mandy turned.

"Where are you going?" Abby asked her.

"I'm just going to make coffee."

"Not by yourself, you're not," Abby said with a shake of her head. "Take two people with you, but wait until the men get back."

I wondered why Abby had snapped at Mandy like that. Perhaps she suspected that one of us, rather than Bazza, was the murderer.

I jumped when Michael and Owen burst into the dining room, worry etched on their faces.

"Bazza's gone!" Michael exclaimed.

"What do you mean 'gone'?" Abby asked.

"Gone," Owen said. "He forced the door open."

Abby clutched her throat. "But how?"

"It seems he used a wrench," Owen said. "Someone gave him a wrench." He and Michael looked at Lisa.

"I didn't give him a wrench," she said. "I wouldn't even know where to find one."

"There was no wrench left in the room, so he's taken it with him, but the marks on the door are obvious," Michael said. "And there was a kitchen knife there as well. *Someone* has given him a kitchen knife to try, and then a wrench."

"You don't know he's a criminal," Lisa said angrily. "You should never have locked him up there in the first place."

"You're very quick to jump to his defence," Vanessa said. "I think we need to lock Lisa up now, in some other room if the lock on that room is broken now. Obviously, she was the one who gave him the wrench so he could free himself from the room. She was the only one left here, and it couldn't have been any of us because we were all together. She's the only one who could have done it." Vanessa's voice rose to a high pitch.

Lisa's face flushed beet red. "But you keep saying there's someone else on the island, someone wandering around loose. How do you know it wasn't that person?"

"So you're saying that Bazza's innocent, but you're saying the murderer broke into the resort to release him?" Vanessa said. "Why would the murderer release an innocent person? Lisa, you'd better get your story straight. There's no point lying. We all know it was you."

Lisa pointed at Vanessa. "She's the murderer!

She's the murderer for sure! She was with Sarah when Sarah was murdered. And just because you all didn't know Bazza was on the island, you said he must be the murderer, but it's obvious it's Vanessa. Why can't you all see that? And I saw Vanessa arguing with Sarah. Didn't you all hear at dinner how Benedict told Sarah he was going to give her a big scoop on someone? Well, that person surely was Vanessa! Benedict knew Vanessa's family and he must've remembered something bad about her and was going to tell Sarah. That's why Benedict was murdered. It all fits! And Laura was murdered only because she was with Benedict at the time. Vanessa had the motive to kill both Benedict and Sarah."

Everyone looked at Vanessa, who sighed. "I'll tell you my story, but I need a glass of wine first."

Michael obliged by pouring her a glass. He offered one to all of us, but we all declined and helped ourselves to water instead.

Vanessa sighed again. "It's a horrible, long story," she said. "I had a sister, Victoria. We had no siblings, and our parents died in a car wreck when we were teenagers. I went to Oxford University, and met my husband there. He was a professor, a much older man, and he died one night of natural causes. It was most unexpected." She paused at this point to dab at her eyes, but I could see they were completely dry. Call me cynical. She pressed on. "Without going into all the details, Victoria became unbalanced. She was always unhappy, because my parents favoured me, to be honest. Anyway, I was the heir to my husband's fortune, and I'd lost touch with Victoria, who had fallen into poverty after becoming addicted to prescription drugs. She contacted me and said she wanted to meet, so I invited her to a spa by the sea in Essex. We had a good time and reconnected nicely, but I had no idea that she was going to kill herself. Looking back, I can see that she wanted to reconcile before she committed suicide, and at the inquest, the psychiatrist said she'd mentioned that, too. If only I'd known that at the time. She threw herself off a cliff on the last day we were at the spa."

Vanessa stood and crossed her arms. "Benedict thought I was my sister, that's all. My sister and I were only a year apart in age. I myself had never met Benedict, but my sister mentioned him." She snorted rudely. "Benedict and my sister went to Cambridge University together for a semester, if I remember correctly, then my sister needed surgery and dropped out after that. You can see why

Benedict got an awful shock to see me. He must've thought he'd seen a ghost. And if Benedict was talking to Sarah about me, then it would have been over the fact that my poor sister threw herself to her death from the cliffs. It was all over the papers in England at the time, so it's hardly a scoop. Anyway Lisa, you're only saying that to throw suspicion off yourself. I saw *you* have quite a nasty argument with Benedict."

"You're lying!" Lisa said. "*You're* the one who's saying that to throw suspicion off *yourself*. You're the murderer!"

Owen held up his hands. "Everyone calm down. Tempers are running high, which is understandable due to the circumstances, but it doesn't help."

"Are you going to lock her up?" Vanessa asked.

"I might just as easily lock *you* up," Owen said. "Everyone here is a suspect, and so is Bazza, but he's missing now." He shot Lisa a look as he said it. "All we can do is stay calm and wait for the police. They'll be here as soon as the storm breaks. Meanwhile, we all have to stick together. We don't have any other options. And now, let's all prepare dinner."

Vanessa stomped her foot. "You need to lock

Lisa up!" she screeched. "She let that pool boy go, and you're not punishing her. She's probably a murderer, too."

Michael moved to Vanessa and put his hand under her elbow. At first, I thought she would kick him, but she stood still. "Come on, Vanessa," Michael said soothingly. "You've had a fright. Sit down and I'll pour you a nice glass of wine. We can't go accusing each other, because any one of us could be the murderer. We can't go and lock everyone up, now can we?"

I thought Vanessa would be affronted by his tone, but she seemed to calm down, much to my surprise. She did keep shooting dagger looks at Lisa, who returned them, but at least the verbal accusations appeared to have ceased.

CHAPTER 13

"That's ghastly!"

I swung around to see what Lisa was complaining about. I hadn't prepared anything yet, so she couldn't be talking about my cooking.

She was pointing to my blisters. I had removed my shoes, and was standing barefoot in the kitchen. "They must really hurt."

"They sure do," I said. "I'm going to put more Band-Aids on them later, but I'm airing them for now. Going up the hill and back twice in one day in soaking wet shoes did it."

"My feet are sore, too," Mandy piped up.

"You ladies should buy quality shoes," Vanessa said haughtily. "I don't have that problem."

I resisted the urge to strangle Vanessa, and turned my attention to Abby.

"We're cutting corners tonight," Abby said. "Obviously, we can't carry on with the scheduled lessons. This evening, we'll just make pizzas. We will start with the dough."

I wondered if I should ask her if I could just add the toppings, and avoid making the base. It seemed like a good idea to me. By the time I had plucked up the courage to do so, it was already too late.

Abby said something about combining flour, sugar, and yeast in a bowl, but I was too tense to concentrate. Was Bazza the murderer? Was that him I had seen up the hill? Or was it someone else?

There was no way of knowing. The murderer could be someone in the room with me right now, and likely was. I was so deep in thought that it took me a moment or two to note that Abby was speaking to me. "No, you're supposed to knead it lightly, Amelia, not try to kill it." She gasped when she realised what she had said. "Did you remember to add the salt?"

"Yes," I said. "I think so. I hope so."

Abby narrowed her eyes and went onto the next person. "That's an unusual kneading technique, Lisa. No, it's fine." She returned to the front of the room. "Now, as this is a beginners' cooking lesson, I will show you a quick and easy pizza recipe. This is in case you have guests coming and don't have time to let the dough rise for an hour and a half. I want you all to put your dough in the mixing bowl and cover it with cling wrap. Leave it over there in the warm spot for thirty minutes, and while we're waiting for it to rise, we will prepare the toppings."

We all placed our bowls in the place indicated by Abby, and then returned to the benches. "Everyone go to the pantry and collect cheese. There is a selection of cheese, so feel free to use whatever you want. Just be creative. There's mozzarella, Parmesan, Gruyere, ricotta—in fact there's a whole selection of cheeses. Please all go to the pantry now and select your toppings."

Everyone raced to the pantry as if they were entrants on *MasterChef.* I selected some tomatoes, baby spinach, olives, and feta cheese. I thought it best to keep it simple. The others returned to the kitchen laden with spinach, pesto, onions, garlic, pineapples and mushrooms, jalapeños, and anchovies.

I cut up my tomatoes, and then stood around

looking bored while the others diced all their ingredients.

After what seemed an age, Abby told us to fetch our pastry. She said to remove it from the bowl and knead it for a minute, roll it into a pizza base shape, and then we would be able to add our toppings. She walked along and inspected each person's in turn. When she got to mine, she stopped and looked at it. She removed the cling wrap and tipped it onto the countertop. It splattered everywhere. Abby appeared lost for words. When she regained her composure, she tried to scoop it up. "I'm afraid it won't do at all, Amelia. Not to worry, there are ready-made pizza bases in the refrigerator. Go and get one, and use that instead."

I was somewhat embarrassed, but it could've been worse. I went to the refrigerator and found a wrapped pizza base. It was even labelled. I read the label five times just to make sure I had not mixed it up with something else, but it definitely said 'pizza base.' I went back to my workstation and added the toppings to it.

Abby instructed us to put our pizzas in the oven, so that is exactly what I did. Everyone else left their benches and chatted, but I kept my eyes on mine for the first few minutes. Nothing untoward happened, so I went to join the others.

The conversation was tense, but at least people weren't accusing each other of murder. There had been no thunder for a while, but the rain was still furiously beating against the windows.

Michael was the first to notice the smell. "What's burning?" he asked.

I immediately went to my oven, and turned it off before opening the door. The most awful smell emanated from it, reminiscent of old socks and dead flesh. Michael pulled me away from the oven. "Don't breathe it in! The fumes would be toxic." He turned on the fan above my oven, and then instructed everyone else to turn on theirs.

Abby turned on the overhead fans in the room. "It's obviously not safe to open the windows," she said, "so everyone, get your pizzas from your ovens as fast as you can and take them to the dining room."

Everyone did as they were told, coughing and spluttering. I apologised at length.

"Don't worry about it," Owen said, glaring at me. "Listen everyone, we can't go back into the teaching kitchen tonight. I'll have to scrape the molten plastic from the bottom of the oven tomorrow."

"Oh, is that what happened?" I asked him as we made our way from the kitchen.

"Yes," he said through gritted teeth. "You didn't remove the plastic base that was under the pizza before you put it in the oven."

I slapped myself on the side of the head. "I didn't even know it had one! No wonder it smelled so bad."

No one spoke to me again until we were in the dining room. Everyone cut their pizzas into pieces and distributed them around the table, so at least I had plenty to eat. I did feel a little guilty about eating the pizzas that everyone else had made after nearly causing a large-scale environmental disaster, but they didn't seem to mind sharing, so I wasn't going to decline. They probably just wanted to make sure I didn't go back into the kitchen in search of food.

I also felt a little bad about how good everyone else's pizza tasted. They had all made them so easily and they turned out so well that I had to wonder if I was the only actual beginner here. I mean, I was arguably on a level lower than 'beginner,' but everybody else seemed so confident

I couldn't help but wonder why they'd bother coming to a cooking class at all. I was becoming more certain that this was all a front for *a good time*, as some liked to call it.

Everybody ate in silence, which did precious little to soothe my nerves and my embarrassment at yet another cooking failure. I thought that maybe I should be proud that I had managed to do as well as I did, since it was a vast improvement, but it still wasn't exactly what I'd call a success.

After dinner, we continued to sit silently. Nobody moved or spoke for several minutes, which I assumed was because nobody wanted to go back to their room. I knew that I didn't, at least. The thought of being alone was less than comforting, even if it was fairly secure.

Michael sighed loudly before speaking. "I suppose we should go to bed, then. Need to be up early for breakfast," he said, managing a weak smile. Everybody murmured their agreement and stood up. I followed suit, not looking forward to another restless night.

Owen and Abby led me back to my room, waiting with me as I checked every nook and cranny for intruders. After a couple of minutes of searching, I turned back to the door. "Thanks for waiting," I said.

"Oh, that's fine," Abby replied with a tight smile. "Can't be too careful, I suppose. We'll come and collect you early tomorrow. Don't leave your room until you hear both of us at the door."

I nodded. "Don't worry, I definitely don't plan to." The idea of staying in my secure room was scary enough, so I absolutely had no intention of wandering around the halls at night.

Abby and Owen bid me goodnight and headed back to the dining room to escort the others. I locked the door behind them, checking three times to make sure it was secure. I glanced around the room to see if there was anything I had overlooked that could be used to secure the door, but came up empty again.

The door was thick and heavy, and the latch strong, so it was unlikely that anybody would be able to break through it. If anyone did manage to steal a set of keys, they wouldn't be able to get in, due to the latch.

My heart jumped as I remembered that I hadn't latched the sliding door. I ran over to it and sighed with relief to see it was still latched tightly from the previous night. That made sense, I thought, since I had no reason to unlatch it. It was not as secure, because anyone skilled would be able to open it with a knife. I could only hope nobody would try.

The storm had subsided to some degree, but heavy wind and rain still pelted the island, and my window was all that stood between me and the wild elements of nature.

I peered out through the window and looked over the island. It would surely be beautiful in nicer weather and without a murderer on the loose, I thought, before I realised how obvious that was.

Just as I moved to turn away, I glimpsed something outside. I peered closer, my face all but pressed against the glass. In the distance, I saw something moving around in the storm. My first thought was that it was something that had blown loose in the wind, but after a few moments I noticed that it was moving quite distinctly. It was a person.

Somebody, for whatever reason, was walking around outside in the storm. Could it have been Bazza? I shuddered at the thought of a killer silently moving around without a care for the storm, waiting for their moment. The glare from the light in my room was making it harder to see exactly who was out there, and I quickly figured out that it made me very easy to see in turn.

I hurried back to turn off the light, and then raced back to the window. Whoever had been outside was gone, any trace that they had been there, gone with them. I stood alone in the dark and shivered, hugging myself tightly.

Logically, I knew I was safe in the room. There was no way anybody could get through my door short of a battering ram, but the thought of a killer stalking around in the rain was more than I could handle. I huddled up tightly under my blanket and tried to fall asleep.

I closed my eyes tightly and tried to concentrate on the sound of the rain hitting the window. It had always relaxed me before, but the storm was still severe enough that the sound put me on edge. I thought of Ruprecht, Camino, Thyme, and Mint, and wondered what they were all doing at that moment. Of course, I also thought of Alder, and my last thoughts before I fell asleep were of him.

CHAPTER 14

I awoke to the familiar sound of rain driving angrily against the window. I was relieved that I hadn't been murdered in my sleep, of course, but was still embarrassed about burning the pizza base in the kitchen last night. Then again, that was probably the least embarrassing cooking incident I'd ever had, so maybe it was a sign that I was improving.

I stretched and yawned, wincing in pain as the blisters on my feet stung. They had improved considerably overnight, but weren't exactly healed. I just hoped we wouldn't have to climb the hill again. It wasn't just the pain, but the thought of travelling through those tunnels gave me chills.

Every time we had, we'd returned to something awful.

The latest was that Bazza, the mysterious pool boy, had escaped his captivity. Apparently with help, no less. It seemed unlikely that anybody would have freed him unless they were partners in crime, since if he'd just been left in his cell, then the police could have sorted it out with him. Similarly, it was hard to believe he would want to be out of a secure room with a murderer on the loose.

I gingerly stepped out of bed and shuffled over to the window, placing my hand against the cool glass. The storm was unrelenting. The palm trees were bent over nearly halfway and the waves were enormous. The rain had not let up in the least. There was no way the police could traverse this to reach us any time soon.

Before I could step away from the window, something darted past my peripheral vision. It was too fast to tell for certain, but it seemed as if somebody was again outside in the storm. Could Owen have been out doing something to the generator? Would Bazza have risked it in daylight? Was there someone on the island we didn't even know about? Or had I just imagined it? I certainly hadn't imagined it the previous night.

My temples throbbed. This was way too much for me to handle. I had been stressed that this was a cooking resort, but in hindsight I'd have preferred to burn a meal every day rather than have to put up with the knowledge that a murderer was on the loose. Then again, this way I got to worry about a murderer *and* burn a meal every day.

A knock sounded on the door, causing me to jump. "Amelia, are you awake?" a familiar voice asked. It was Abby.

"I'm here as well," Owen's voice added, so I knew it was safe to open the door. As I walked towards the door, I briefly considered that maybe they were in on it together, but it seemed unlikely, especially after what I had seen between Abby and Michael.

The door opened and, to my relief, Abby and Owen were standing calmly and patiently.

"Sorry," I said half heartedly. "Slow start this morning."

"Don't worry about it," Abby said. "I can understand not being especially enthused about starting the day."

"For what it's worth, the storm seems to be dying down," Owen said, though it was hard to believe after what I had just seen out the window. I remembered seeing a figure outside and noticed that Owen was bone dry. Whoever was out there, it hadn't been him, unless he had quickly changed and towelled off. But, no, that would be impossible. He had knocked only moments after I had seen the figure.

"I think I saw somebody out there just now," I said, gesturing to the window.

"What? In the storm?" Owen asked with a raised eyebrow. When I nodded in response, he hesitated for a moment before speaking. "Are you positive? It's dying down, but it could still easily blow somebody over. At any rate, the others have already gathered in the dining room."

I sighed and rubbed my head. "No, I guess I'm not positive. I'm fairly sure I did." My voice trailed off away. "I'm sure I did see someone out there last night."

"Well, let's get some breakfast. If somebody was out there today, they'll be soaking wet, so they'll be easy to spot. It's more likely the stress is just getting to you," Abby suggested. The thought wasn't exactly encouraging. Still, I supposed it was better than a mysterious stranger running about.

The three of us walked wordlessly to the dining room together. I glanced around the room, doing a quick head count. It seemed we were short one person, Michael. Before I could ask where he was, Lisa spoke up.

"Good morning, Amelia. Michael's just gone to check on the cool room. When he gets back, we're going to make omelettes," she said with a forced smile.

I felt my stomach twist into a knot. I could barely believe they were still letting me cook. Every other time had been an unmitigated disaster. My best hope was that I'd manage to cause so much damage to the kitchen that we wouldn't be able to use it again. I sighed, wishing there was some kind of super pizza delivery service that could reach us through the storm.

"How was everybody's night?" Owen asked, as he took a seat and looked around the table. Lisa shrugged silently, and nobody else so much as reacted.

"Fine, I guess," I said, just to break the silence. "I did see someone outside last night, but I couldn't make out who it was."

"Oh, that reminds me," Owen said, interrupting me. "Has anybody been outside today?"

"Out in the storm?" Vanessa said in an insufferably smug tone. "Of course not. What reason would we have? Do you think somebody's going to try to swim back to shore?" she asked sarcastically. I couldn't help but wish she would try.

"Just wondering," Owen said, leaning back in his chair and sighing.

A few more minutes passed without anybody uttering a single word. The wind was still howling outside as the rain beat against the windows, threatening to burst inside. I knew the windows were latched, but it was still hard to believe they were sufficiently sturdy to withstand the viciousness of the storm. I was about to comment on it just to start a conversation, when Michael burst into the room.

"Bad news," he said simply, causing my heart to sink. I couldn't imagine what news could be considered 'bad' given our recent circumstances, but I assumed it wasn't that the mini bar wasn't going to be restocked. "I've just been to the cool room, and the murder weapons are missing."

The room collectively gasped. My heart and

mind raced. Who could have done it? Michael could have, certainly. It was also his idea to put them there in the first place, which he could have suggested just so he would be able to collect them later. But then, why announce it to us all? That didn't add up. Who else could have taken them?

"That's not all," Michael continued. "The bag with Vanessa's shirt has been taken, too."

The entire room turned to look at Vanessa, who had gone pale. "Well, it obviously wasn't me!" she yelled. "Why would I give it to you willingly and then steal it back? It so obviously points to me."

Owen nodded. "That makes sense," he said with a sigh, obviously overlooking the fact that Vanessa had been far from willing to surrender her shirt. "It would be stupid to steal evidence that pointed to you. All that does is create even more suspicion."

Michael cleared his throat. "I'm not done yet," he announced, to which the room collectively groaned. How could this get any worse?

"I found wrench marks on the cool room door. That was how the door was opened. It must have been Bazza, as we already know he has a wrench. We won't be able to use it as a secure room any more," Michael explained with a pained look.

"Mind if I have a look?" Owen stood up as he asked Michael. "It's not that I don't trust you, but none of us can be sure unless two people have seen it. Take me to it and we'll be back in no time." Michael nodded and the two walked off towards the cool room.

"It's obvious you did it," Lisa snarled at Vanessa. "None of us are falling for it."

"Back off!" Vanessa said viciously. "Why would I steal my own shirt back? That would just make me more suspicious. I bet you did it just to frame me."

"Oh, as if!" Lisa stood up suddenly, knocking her chair aside. "You have the knives, too, I bet. Well, I'm not going anywhere alone with you."

"Calm down, you two," Abby said with a sigh. "Michael and Owen won't be gone long. Let's start breakfast."

I felt my stomach twist into a knot all over again. I almost preferred people accusing each other of murder to having to try to cook an omelette. I sighed, preparing myself for the worst. To look on the bright side, I had caused slightly less damage with each attempt, so maybe this time I'd only start a small fire.

We all gathered in the teaching kitchen, where Abby explained the process to us as usual. She laid out the ingredients in front of us as she spoke. "Today, we're just making a simple cheese, ham, and tomato omelette. It should be quite foolproof," she muttered, giving me a pointed look. I knew I'd prove her wrong, willingly or not.

For the first time since I'd arrived, I was thankful for the storm raging outside. If I did manage to start a fire, at least it wouldn't be able to spread far, though I didn't much enjoy the thought of huddling in the tunnels while we looked sadly back at the burned remains of the resort.

I swallowed hard and looked down at my ingredients. Eggs, a tomato, some cheese, slices of ham, milk, butter and a small assortment of herbs. Everybody else was either finely dicing their tomatoes with impeccable skill or already whisking a mixture together.

"You can sit this one out if you'd like, Amelia," Abby said with a hopeful smile. It took all the willpower I had to turn her down, knowing that I had to improve, even if it meant causing one disaster after another. Abby slinked away sadly, probably going to stand by the nearest fire exit, or so I thought.

I followed the written instructions as closely as I could. I turned on the hotplate, whisked the eggs with salt and pepper, and reluctantly poured it into the preheated pan. To my relief nothing exploded or caught fire, and seemed to be going very well.

The tomato didn't take long to dice, and then I scattered some herbs, tomato and cheese throughout the mixture as it cooked.

"Amelia!" Abby screamed, running towards me. I turned back to see that my omelette had turned a dark brown, almost black, as Abby grabbed the frying pan and took it off the hotplate.

"What happened?" I asked sadly.

"You had the hotplate up way too high!" she said, exasperated.

"Too high?" I shrugged. "I didn't think the hotplate could be lowered," I said, wondering how it worked. It seemed to me that everybody else's hotplate was sitting on top of the stove just like mine was.

CHAPTER 15

"I don't see why we all have to go up that stupid hill again," Vanessa said for the fifth time. "I'm sure that stupid pool boy won't come back. Why don't half of you go out and leave the other half of us here?"

The normally unflappable Michael sighed and rubbed his eyes. "We don't know if Bazza actually *is* the murderer," he said, "as we have already discussed. It could be one of us. If it *is* one of us, then it's not safe to leave that person with just one other person. That is precisely why we go to all the trouble of escorting everyone to their rooms of a night and collecting everyone from their rooms of a morning." He said it very slowly as if speaking to a particularity irritating and slow-to-understand child.

"Well, I don't like it!" she said. "My feet hurt. I can't go out there again!"

"Surely your high quality shoes haven't hurt your feet?" I said snarkily. I was completely over her whining and complaining. We were all in the same boat, so to speak. Everyone was tense, but everyone else was doing their best to make it bearable.

She shot me a look of pure malice. "It's just stupid. It's just a stupid idea for all of us to go up the hill. What is this? The third time up the hill? If we hadn't gone up the hill, then Sarah would still be alive."

"We had to speak with the police," Owen said wearily. "And now we need to find out from the police if Bazza has a criminal record."

Vanessa held up her hands. "And if you find out that he's a murderer, what will you do then? You will rest easy because you'll know it's him? Is that what you were about to say?" She put her hands on hips and jutted out her jaw.

"Look, Vanessa," Michael said in a conciliatory tone, but I could tell he was reaching the end of his patience, "there have been no murders since we've all gone everywhere together and stuck together. And while I could suggest locking you in your room, I don't think that will be safe. Sure, we allowed Lisa to remain behind in her room, but that was before Bazza escaped."

"I didn't let him out!" Lisa said, not at all convincingly.

I rubbed my temples. This was all so stressful. It seemed obvious to me that Lisa had helped Bazza escape, but I had no idea why. I certainly didn't want to go up the hill again listening to Vanessa complaining incessantly, and worse still, my heels were red raw. I was dreading the thought of shoes. Thank goodness I had plenty of Band-Aids. Still, Michael was right—we all did have to stick together. It was the only way to stay safe. And what Michael did not say, but I had already realised, is that if the police said Bazza did not have a criminal record, and had no connection to any of the guests, that meant it was far more likely, even certain, that one of us was the murderer. We did need to hear what the police had uncovered.

This time, going up the hill had the added threat that Bazza was out there somewhere on the island. He could be waiting in ambush, but he was unlikely to take on a group of people.

Owen stopped to talk to us before we went into the tunnel. "Listen up everyone, I'm sure I don't need to tell you to be alert. Very alert. If anyone sees Bazza, call out to let the rest of us know immediately. I'm sure there's no way he'll let himself be seen, so for that reason he'll pose no threat to us, so long as we all stick together. It's very important that we do stick close and keep our eyes open. I doubt he'll be hiding in the tunnel, because he'll expect us to go up the hill again to get mobile phone service. He wants to keep out of our way even more than we want to keep out of his."

I sure hoped that was true.

"We're going to do things a little differently this time," Owen continued. "I'm going to go at the front, and Michael will bring up the rear. You're all to make very certain that you stay between the two of us. Is that understood?"

Everyone readily agreed. I thought that was a smart move. If Bazza was the killer, and Lisa was in it with him, then Lisa couldn't drop behind and do anything that would escape the notice of the others. It seemed like a good plan.

For the third, and what I hoped was the last, time I entered the tunnel. I felt safer this time than previously, as the whole group was there. Yet once again, I felt exposed somehow in the dank confines of the tunnel.

As we walked through the tunnel, I ran the problem through my mind. Was Bazza the murderer and acting in combination with Lisa? And what motive could they have had for killing Benedict and Laura, or Sarah for that matter? Or was Bazza acting alone? Did Lisa have a crush on him and so was blissfully unaware that he had committed murder? That seemed the more likely option. And then there was Vanessa, who had fallen behind at the very time Sarah was murdered. Was that simply a coincidence? Or had the chef stayed on the island?

And Owen and Michael seemed awfully friendly. Were they the perpetrators? For the third time, I approached the end of the tunnel and saw the chopping block. This time, Owen stopped and manoeuvred the axe out of the block of wood.

My heart sank to my stomach. Could Owen be the murderer? Was he about to attack us, swinging the axe? I experienced a moment of pure terror.

Owen looked back over his shoulder. "I should've got this the last time. It's unwise leaving it out in the open, and I'm surprised Bazza hasn't taken it by now. If we do run into Bazza, it'll be good to have this axe." With that, Owen took off and ran for the next tunnel.

The storm had definitely abated. The rain was only half strength now and the wind was nowhere near as violent. That meant the police would be here soon. I nearly cried with relief, but I still had to keep myself safe until they arrived.

Halfway up the stairs, my heels started to hurt again. I reached down and could feel the Band-Aids had worked their way off. I had brought extra Band-Aids in my pocket, but I would have to wait until I was at the top of the hill to stick them on.

When we emerged from the tunnel and climbed up the short outcrop of rocks to the clearing, I saw at once that I had service on my phone. I immediately received a bunch of texts, some from Thyme, some from Ruprecht, and all the rest from Alder.

Owen was already speaking into his phone, hopefully to the police. What if this was all a front and he had never actually contacted the police? My heart beat out of my chest. I forced my attention to the others. Some were speaking, while others were thumbing through their phones.

Ruprecht and Thyme had both texted me to

say they were doing spells for my protection, and while Alder had said that too, he had also sent me screenshots of various news articles. I quickly saved them one by one onto my phone so I could look at them later. By the time I had saved the last photo, Owen was gathering everyone, telling us all to go down the rocky outcrop to the tunnel. I was disappointed that I hadn't had time to call Alder, but at least I had saved all the photos he had sent me, and could read them at my leisure. Once again Owen organised us to follow him, with Michael bringing up the rear.

"It's obvious to all of us that the storm is nowhere near as bad as it was," Owen said, "and that means the police will soon be on their way. This means that Bazza will be more desperate, so keep an eye out for him."

"What did the police say about him?" Lisa asked.

"I'll tell you all about it when we're safely back inside," Owen said. He shot Michael a significant look which I interpreted to mean he was asking him to keep a close eye on Lisa. I hoped so, anyway.

We all made it down the steps safely enough, though I had not had a chance to replace the

Band-Aids on my heels, and my feet were awfully painful. Nevertheless, I sprinted across the area between the tunnels just as fast as ever. If Bazza was going to ambush us, that was surely where he would do it.

Just then, I noticed a sheltered rocky outcrop not too far from the break in the tunnels.

CHAPTER 16

I hadn't even been able to see it before with the driving rain, but now that the storm was clearing, it was visible. I wondered if Bazza was sheltering there, and for a moment, hesitated to mention it. After all, Owen and Abby had to know it was there, and they had not commented on it, for whatever reason. I wondered whether it was best to stay out of it, but then decided against it.

I called out to Owen as soon as I reached the other tunnel.

He stopped at once. "Is everything okay?"

"There's a sort of shelter out there between the tunnels. I wondered if Bazza might be hiding in it."

"The shelter?" Abby said. "Oh yes, it's…" Her voice trailed away. I couldn't see her expression in the dark.

"Shouldn't we go and check it out?" I asked them.

Against Lisa's protests, we all hurried to the shelter and then crowded under the rocky outcrop. "It looks like Bazza has indeed been in here," Michael said. There were empty bottles of gin lying on the ground. The outcrop provided a good shelter from the elements, and the ground was soft and sandy.

"Bazza or someone else," I said. "Are you sure no one else is hiding on the island?"

Abby and Owen hurried to assure me that no one else was, but I had my doubts. "No point staying around here," Owen said. "Bazza isn't here now, and it's best if we avoid him, at any rate. Let's get back."

We hurried through the tunnel once more, again in single file.

When we made it back to the office, I let out a long sigh of relief that I would never have to set foot inside those tunnels again. While they were mercifully wide and high tunnels, they were still filled with stale air, and goodness knows what manner of creepy crawly.

Owen led us all to the dining room and indicated we should sit. He remained standing. "The police have said that Bazza does indeed have a criminal record." Lisa gasped, but Owen kept talking. "He's not wanted for murder, or anything like that, more like charges to do with drug possession."

"Did the police think he could have been the murderer?" I asked him.

Owen shrugged. "They didn't tell me, but they just said he had no arrests for violence."

"I told you so!" Lisa said.

I thought she wasn't being very wise. If anyone had any doubts that she had released Bazza from his prison, then I don't think they would have any now.

"That means the murderer is someone in this room," Lisa added.

Owen held up his hands. "Now, let's not jump to any conclusions. The police will be here soon, so let's leave it to them. Meanwhile, we should all stick closely together. We'll follow the same protocol as usual, with Abby and I escorting everyone to their rooms."

When I reached the safety of my room and locked the door, I thought about staying there until the police arrived. I peeped out the sliding doors, and for the first time since the storm hit, I could see the ocean, albeit through a haze of rain.

I decided to have a hot shower, but instead of languishing under it, I would hurry to see what Alder had sent me. I'd had a quick skim through the photos and found nothing of interest, but I hadn't had a chance to study them thoroughly.

Once under the hot water, I was tempted to linger, but those photos were beckoning to me. I dried myself rapidly and threw on some clothes, and then hurried into the bedroom. I held the curtains back for another peep through the window, and saw with delight that the storm had almost gone. The torrential rain had lifted, and I could see the ocean clearly. Large quantities of driftwood had washed up on the beach and the sea still looked wild, but now the police would be on their way. I felt like cheering.

I threw myself back on the bed and scrolled through the photos on my phone. They were mostly newspaper clippings. I had originally texted Alder the name of each person who was here, and the names of people who were murdered, to see if he could find any connection. His brief message stated that he had drawn a blank. He couldn't see any connection between the hosts, the guests, and the murder victims, but said that he was sending me screenshots of all the relevant newspaper articles he had found.

The first article was from a newspaper at the Sunshine Coast. It was written by a travel journalist who had spent time at Paradise Island Cooking School, doing the Beginners' Classes. I was surprised at first, and then amused, as the journalist said that it was nothing more than a Swingers' Club. That certainly explained a lot. I had seen Abby and Michael kissing passionately, and it was surely clear to everyone that there was something between them. I also rather suspected there was something going on between Owen and Mandy. And then there was Lisa, who had a crush on, if not a relationship with, Bazza the pool boy. Even with the seriousness of the situation, I could not resist a chuckle. What would my friends think when I told them they had sent me to such a place?

There were several screenshots of old newspaper articles about the island, but I couldn't see anything that would be of any help. The next one was one about Bazza, a brief article saying he had been convicted of a drug possession charge, but was let off on a good behaviour bond. That was the only newspaper article about Bazza.

I thought it would be nice to sit and look through the screenshots that Alder had sent me, while facing the view I had been unable to see for days. The only view previously had been a wall of water. With that in mind, I crossed the room, and my hand reached for the curtain.

I pulled back the curtain, and screamed in shock.

CHAPTER 17

Bazza's face was pressed against the window, and Owen was right behind him. It took me a while to realise that Owen was trying to get Bazza in an arm lock. I was terrified, and could only watch helplessly as Bazza aimed a blow at Owen's head. Owen missed, but in his manoeuvre to avoid Bazza's punch, lost his balance and stumbled backwards.

I watched Bazza sprint down the beach with Owen hard on his heels.

I unlocked my door and called out for help. No one came, so I ran down the corridor to the dining room where the others were gathered. "Quick! Owen and Bazza are struggling outside!" I yelled.

Michael was already half way to the door. "All of you wait here," he said over his shoulder.

"What was Owen doing outside?" Vanessa asked Abby.

"Owen went to turn the generator off, given that the storm's all but gone now." Abby's face was white, and she was shaking.

"I'm sure Owen will be all right," I said. "He had Bazza's arm behind his back, but Bazza got away."

I could see Lisa was agitated. I had forgotten for a moment that she had something going on with Bazza. Lisa sprinted to the window. She struggled to open the shutters, but Abby hurried over to help her. "We can have the shutters open now," Abby said, as she set about opening them.

A collective gasp went up as we looked out the window. Michael and Owen had Bazza between them. He was throwing punches wildly, but the two men appeared to be getting the better of him.

They finally overcame him, and dragged him towards the door. Lisa protested loudly as they pushed Bazza inside the room.

"What are you going to do with him?" Vanessa asked. "I assume there's no lock on that door now, what with him using a wrench to get it open. Do you have another room you could use?"

"I haven't done anything wrong," Bazza said.

Lisa hurried to his side. "That's right! He hasn't!"

Michael blocked her, and pushed Bazza into a chair. He and Owen stood either side of him.

"He did it for sure," Owen said. "I was out at the generator shed and I saw smoke. I went to investigate and saw Bazza standing over a small fire. In it was a shirt, or rather, its remains. The two knives were there, too, in the fire. He must have been trying to burn the evidence."

"I saw the smoke and went to investigate, too," Bazza said. His eyes darted wildly around the room. He was hunched over and shaking. Stubble covered his face. He looked dirty and as if he was barely hanging onto the last vestiges of his sanity. He smelled strongly of gin—I could smell it from where I was standing several feet away. I had seen the empty gin bottles under the rocky outcrop. His eyes rolled and I thought he was going to faint, yet he suddenly jerked to attention. "It wasn't my shirt," he said. "It was a woman's shirt. I wondered who was burning it."

"Was it a woman's shirt?" I asked Owen.

Owen shrugged. "No idea. I only saw the remains of it. It was almost burned through by the time I got there."

"Did you put out the fire?" Abby snapped at him. "The police might be able to extract some sort of evidence from it."

Owen's face flushed. "In case you hadn't noticed, I had my hands full chasing Bazza. Once I spotted him, I thought it better to chase him than to preserve evidence for the police." He almost spat the words.

"Why did you kill them?" Michael asked Bazza. "What did you have against Benedict and Laura, or Sarah for that matter?"

Bazza rocked backwards and forwards on his chair. "I didn't kill anyone." His speech was slurred. "I didn't kill anyone."

"Stop! Can't you see you're upsetting him?" Lisa burst into tears.

Abby took her by the arm and tried to steer her away from Bazza, but Lisa would have none of it. "He didn't kill anyone!" she said. "It's that French chef. He always *was* strange. I bet he's out running around the island now, and if it's not him, it's one of us."

Michael ignored her. "Owen, can you go and

get some rope to tie him up? And Lisa, don't even think about releasing him this time. He's definitely the murderer, and we'll have to leave it to the police to deal with him."

Owen hurried from the room, but my attention remained on Bazza. He was shaking so violently now that his feet tapped an erratic rhythm on the floor.

"You can't tie him up!" Lisa shrieked. "He hasn't done anything wrong. It's just a coincidence that he was standing over the burning shirt and the um, knives." Her voice trailed away and I wondered for a moment if she was actually beginning to doubt his story.

"Vanessa's shirt was there in the cool room with the knives as well," Lisa continued. "You don't know that Bazza was burning his own shirt! In fact, he said he wasn't burning anything at all. He only went to see what the smoke was. And Owen said he went to see what the smoke was too, and you don't suspect him of anything."

Mandy placed her hand on Lisa's shoulder. "Lisa, I know you don't want to believe it, but please see how it looks. Bazza was the one who murdered Sarah, and the others. We just don't know why. Maybe the police can get it out of him."

Lisa burst into tears and ran from the room. Abby made to go after her.

"Let her go," Michael said. "So long as she doesn't untie him, she won't do any harm. She won't be in any danger now if she runs off by herself, because we've caught the killer. We'll stay with Bazza until the police come, but he's either inebriated or stoned, so I doubt he'll give us any more trouble."

Vanessa sank into a chair. "I'm so glad this whole nightmare's over now."

"I wonder what his motive could possibly be?" I said to nobody in particular.

"Those three guests were very rude to him," Abby said. "It's hard to deal with the public all the time. Even 'people persons' begin to resent people once they've had to deal with the public for any length of time. Perhaps they were so rude to him that they pushed him over the edge. Who knows?"

Owen returned with a length of rope, but at that moment, a gust of wind blew the door open. Perhaps Michael and Owen hadn't shut it properly when they had come in, as they'd had their hands full with Bazza. As Abby went to shut it, a huge rat ran into the room. It twitched its large nose and ran in circles, making a horrible squealing sound. Vanessa screamed at the top of her lungs, while the rest of us took evasive action.

Bazza took advantage of the situation and sprinted out the door, with Owen and Michael hard on his heels. Lisa ran after them, screaming at them.

Michael and Owen returned only moments later with the unfortunate Bazza, who already had his hands tied behind his back with rope. They brought him inside and wrapped more rope around him, securing him to the chair.

"Where's Lisa?" Abby asked them.

"She's out there sitting at the beach, crying," Michael said.

Abby nodded. "I'll go after her."

I was more interested to know where the huge rat had gone. It was the biggest rat I had ever seen. In fact, I didn't know rats could grow that big.

Mandy apparently was thinking the same thing. "Did you see the size of that rat? It looked the size of a small wombat."

"Do you think it was actually a rat?" I asked her.

Owen answered for her. "It's not unusual to

have wildlife try to find shelter during and after a storm. Obviously, the wildlife couldn't get in before because we had everything bolted down in the storm. It's nothing to worry about."

Nothing to worry about? Giant rodents on the loose? Still, I supposed that was better than a murderer on the loose.

CHAPTER 18

$\mathcal{I}$ was beyond relieved that the murderer had been caught. I couldn't wait to find out what had motivated him to go on a killing spree, but I would find out eventually. Now all we had to do was wait for the police to come. The rain had all but stopped, but it looked like it would start again any minute. At any rate, it was no longer storm rain, rather a light drizzle.

The wind, too, had died down. Rather than the gale-force winds that had been slamming the island for days, it was now a gentle, consistent breeze. The clouds still looked fierce, and for a moment I feared that the police would have to turn back before they arrived. I just had to have faith that they knew what they were doing and could time their boat ride to the island. They would certainly know more about this kind of weather than I would, at any rate.

There was still no television reception, and I was afraid that Owen and Abby would suggest cooking lessons. I wondered what I could do to escape that, as I certainly didn't want to make anything else explode. It was then that I thought of the lightning struck wood. It was awfully hard to get, and I had never managed to find any in Bayberry Creek. Ruprecht and the others always sang its praises. They said it added power to every spell, and was better than coffee when speed was needed in a spell. I often added coffee to my spells to hurry along the manifestation I wanted, but lightning struck wood was like coffee on steroids. It was potent stuff indeed, and could be used in a variety of spells, bringing as it did the power of lightning to the spell.

Since lightning had struck the tree at the top of the hill, I was fairly certain it had also struck trees around the resort. I wanted to find such a tree, and take some wood, not only for myself, but also to give as gifts to Ruprecht, Camino, Mint, and of course, Thyme. They would be delighted to have such a gift. I briefly wondered if they would want to give me another gift of my own after their last one had stranded me on the island with a killer. It wasn't in any way their fault, of course, but it had me more than a little bit wary of taking trips anywhere unfamiliar in the future.

I probably only had two hours before the police arrived, so I thought I should make a start. I went to my room, unescorted for the first time in days, and fetched my largest carry bag. When I returned to the dining room, Owen and Mandy were no longer there, and Abby and Lisa were sitting at the dining table. Michael was hovering behind Bazza.

I told Abby and Michael where I was going. "That's a good idea," Abby said. "It's been hard for you all not being able to explore the island. Oh, of course the murders made it hard for everyone. Please forgive me, I'm just so tired and stressed that I don't know what I'm saying."

Michael whispered to me, "You go off and explore, and have a good time, but it's probably best to stay close to the resort. The police will be here presently, in an hour or so. We'll keep an eye on Lisa."

I nodded, my former sunny mood giving way to a moment of disquiet. I had forgotten the possibility that Lisa might have been in it with Bazza.

Still, I would make sure I enjoyed my exploration of the area around the resort. I knew there was the lightning struck tree up the top of the hill, but there was no way I was going to climb the hill one more time, whether by means of the tunnels or not. As a matter of fact, I would have been happy never to hear the word 'tunnel' again.

I could see how beautiful the island would be in good weather. The sea looked angry and was dark and churning, and slender palm trees had washed up on the beach. Their trunks were extraordinarily beautiful shades of lime-green and dark coppery brown. I imagined this was normally a pristine beach, but now it just looked a mess. Swaying palm trees stretched out over the landscape before me, and I suddenly remembered the giant rat. I shuddered, but walked on.

The rain was light, but still enough to be annoying. I squinted as I walked, looking for any sign of a tree that had been struck by lightning. Quite a few had been torn at by the storm, which made me realise that it had been especially intense, even for the island that supposedly had so many.

I continued walking, squinting against the wind

and rain, and soon found what I was looking for. In fact, I had a choice. It looked like the one lightning strike had taken down two trees. They had fallen into the sand, leaving a great dent in the beach. In many ways, it was an intimidating sight, though it did serve as a reminder of the sheer power that lightning possessed. Pieces of wood lay all over on the ground, so I did not even have to go to the effort of breaking any off.

I gleefully collected as much as I could carry, and then sat on the burned tree trunk. I exhaled long and hard, and then shook my arms as if to disperse all my cares and worries. What had been going to be a nice time away—if a cooking school could ever be a nice time for me—had turned into a nightmare. Three people had been murdered, and I still did not even know why. Whatever had possessed Bazza to do such a thing? And was Lisa in it with him? In fact, had Bazza committed the murders at Lisa's request?

I shook my head. No, it was all over now, and the police would soon be dealing with it. My part in the ordeal was over. I had to let it go.

I picked up a piece of lightning struck wood and turned it over in my hand. I could feel the power of lightning in it. I was a Dark Witch, and the others had said my power was growing. I decided I should do a spell with the lightning struck wood, a spell to ease my path, to remove all obstacles in front of me, and to bring me luck, and I would use the lightning struck wood to do it. And what better place to do it than an island which had just been through a tropical storm?

I smiled, and picked up one piece of lightning struck wood, leaving the bag on the ground. The wind was rising, so I would be able to speak the spell at the top of my lungs and no one would hear me. I walked along the narrow trail near the resort, yelling the spell at the top of my lungs. It felt good.

Just as I reached the conclusion of the spell, I came to the end of the trail. I injected as much power into my voice as I could, flung my arms skyward, and concluded the spell.

And now all evil, you must flee!

This is my will, so mote it be!

As my voice reached a high crescendo, I heard something rustling in the bushes below. I looked down rapidly, worried that it was a rat.

There, at my feet, were two people. It took me a while to recognise them, because I had never seen them without their clothes before. It was

Owen and Mandy, as naked as the day they were born, clinging together in the bushes at my feet.

I clamped my hands over my eyes. "I'm so sorry!" I said. "I was just reciting a, um, sonnet. Please go about your business."

With that, I removed my hands from my eyes, clamped them over my mouth, and fled the scene. I was starting to wonder more and more about this cooking school, and if I was the only one out of the loop.

CHAPTER 19

I hurried back to the building, my cheeks burning. I told myself that they would be more embarrassed than I was, but it was little consolation. I decided to stay in my room until the police arrived. No more wandering around the island, not after what had just happened. I wasn't going to risk going back outside at what was clearly a Swingers' Club masquerading as a Cooking School. I just had to find my phone, and then I could go to my room.

"There it is," I said to myself as I walked into the dining room where everyone was gathered.

As I reached for my phone, it made a noise. I almost dropped it with shock. "Finally, service!" I said, much to everyone's delight. Of course, given the way my day was going, the service dropped out before I could get a call out to Alder. "Hold that thought," I added. "It's just dropped out again."

"No matter," Lisa said. "You can be comforted by the fact that you'll soon be off the island with all the mobile phone service you need." She glared at me from under knitted eyebrows, and I supposed she was still furious with all of us for tying up Bazza.

I scrolled down to read Alder's message. He said he was on his way. But to where? I supposed he meant he was on his way to Rockhampton Airport, and we could fly back together. How lovely of him. He had also sent a bunch of new articles. *Oh that's right*, I thought, *he doesn't know the murderer's been caught*. I thumbed across the screen to open the first article, but decided to look later. It no longer mattered. I put my phone down and adjusted the Band-Aids on my heels.

Just then, Mandy and Owen returned, looking rather sheepish. I nodded to them and snatched up my phone, intending to beat a hasty retreat. Vanessa was peering at the screen, much to my annoyance. That was just plain rude.

When I reached my room, I sat on the couch and, having nothing better to do, looked at the articles Alder had sent me. The first article was from a London paper. It was about Victoria Vincent's death. It kept referencing Vanessa's husband, who had been an academic yet at the same time the heir to a sizeable fortune, so I supposed that was why Victoria's death had attracted so much media attention. I read the whole article. It was quite sad. When Victoria and Vanessa started college, their parents died. Victoria became addicted to prescription drugs after her heart surgery, and lost touch with Vanessa. She later wanted to reconcile with her sister. There was a photo of Victoria and a photo of Vanessa, and they did look very much alike. I could see why Benedict had been so shocked when he saw Vanessa, why he had so easily mistaken her for Victoria. I continued to read the article, how Vanessa had married into money and was the only heir to her husband's considerable fortune. I read how Victoria had contacted Vanessa, wanting to reconnect at a well-known spa in Essex, and how Victoria had thrown herself to her death off one of the many cliffs in the area.

I sat bolt upright. My phone clattered to the floor. How could I have been so stupid? The answer was there, right in front of my face.

Now I knew why the three of them had been murdered. Vanessa was, in fact, Victoria. I could see how she did it all now. She must have planned it for ages. The two sisters had no living relatives, so it would have been easy, especially given the fact that they looked so alike. She contacted her wealthy, widowed sister and asked her to meet her at a location known for its dangerous cliffs. She had also seen a psychiatrist for weeks leading up to the event, and professed to suicidal tendencies. She had set it up beautifully, and that day had thrown her sister, Vanessa, off the cliff and assumed her identity.

I should have known when I saw the scar on her chest in the mirror. The subject of Victoria's heart surgery had already been raised. That was why Vanessa—rather, Victoria—had been so worried about us looking at her when she dressed. I had just thought she was overly modest.

Now what to do? The police would be on their way. Should I go out and tell the others? Would they be in any danger from her now? I thought not. She had killed Benedict because he had recognised her, and I remembered him taunt her about it. He had also told Sarah in front of Victoria that he had a scoop for her. Victoria had just taken her chances. It was lucky for her that Bazza had stayed on the island as that had thrown suspicion off her. I expect she hadn't had time to think it through or to plan to any degree. Benedict was about to expose her, so she had to act quickly to silence him. She no doubt suspected he had already told Sarah, so she had to dispose of Sarah as well. And Laura had just been in the wrong place at the wrong time.

Had Vanessa seen the article? She had been looking at my phone just before I had taken it from the table. On second thoughts, I would have to tell everyone at once. I had been ignoring the sound at the sliding door. It was a sound I was used to by now, the wind rattling the door. Only it wasn't the wind.

Victoria burst through the door, a knife in hand. The last time I had seen that knife, it was protruding from either Benedict or Laura's body.

I wasn't shocked. Somehow, deep down on some level, I had been expecting it.

"I know you know it's me," she said. She made to lunge at me, but hesitated. No doubt it was the cascarilla powder and red brick dust just across the doorway. I also had the protective mirror spell facing that door.

Those wards would not physically restrain anyone for long, and for once, my house wasn't able to save me.

Vanessa lunged at me, and in one smooth movement, I snatched up the jar of cascarilla powder and red brick dust and threw the mixture in her face.

"You little witch!" she screeched at me, swinging the knife wildly with one hand, while trying to wipe the substance out of her eyes with the other.

"You don't know the half of it," I said, dodging the knife and hitting her over the head with my bag filled with lightning struck wood. Ruprecht always said that practicality was one half of witchcraft.

She fell to the floor in a crumpled heap. I kicked the knife as far as I could, and then stood back to admire my handiwork. That lightning struck wood sure did pack a punch.

Still, there was no time to stand around congratulating myself. Vanessa was writhing on the ground, clutching her head. I sprinted to the dining room to get help.

"Quick, hurry!" I shrieked. "Vanessa's the murderer. She just tried to kill me. She's in my room." I pointed in the direction of my room, which was quite unnecessary, but I was caught up in the heat of the moment.

Michael took off in the direction of my room with Owen right behind him, thankfully, this time fully clothed.

I showed Abby, Mandy, and Lisa the article on my phone, but before I could explain at any length, the two men returned with Vanessa between them. She was struggling wildly, and saying things I could not repeat.

"She tried to attack me with a knife!" Michael said.

I was filled with remorse. "Oh I'm so sorry," I said. "I should never have left her in there."

Michael waved my concerns away. "What else could you have done? You did the right thing coming to get help."

"Bazza is innocent," I told them. "It was Vanessa all the time. I've got all the evidence on my phone." I swiped until the picture came into view, and handed the phone to Abby. "Pass it around, would you? I figured it all out. She murdered her wealthy sister so she could steal her identity."

Everyone looked shocked. Owen and Mandy

both looked at the phone over Abby's shoulder, murmuring their surprise. Lisa was already trying to untie Bazza. "The ropes are too tight," she said frantically. "Can somebody help me?"

"Go and help her," Abby ordered Owen. "That woman is not Vanessa. This article makes it clear. She's Vanessa's sister, Victoria. I saw the scar on her chest when she was taking off her shirt."

That was news to me. "You did? I did, too, but I didn't put two and two together until I read the article. Benedict recognised her, so that's why she killed him."

"But why did she kill Sarah?" Lisa asked, taking a brief respite from strangling the now-released-but-still-inebriated Bazza in a tight hug.

"Remember over dinner the other night, Benedict told Sarah he had a scoop for her?" I said. Mandy looked doubtful, but the others, apart from Lisa who was otherwise preoccupied, murmured that they did remember. "Vanessa probably thought, and likely rightly so, that Benedict intended to tell Sarah about Vanessa's true identity. Also, when I went up the hill with Vanessa and Sarah, Sarah seemed to be afraid of Vanessa, and didn't try to hide it from her."

"I outsmarted you all," Vanessa snapped. "You're all so stupid that you..."

Everyone flushed red at her ensuing remarks. Michael pushed her down in the chair and tied her up with Bazza's newly vacated ropes.

"Could you put a sock in her mouth?" I asked, and that drew some more unsavoury remarks from Vanessa.

"I'm going to be sick," Bazza said. He staggered outside.

Lisa helped him out. Moments later, she yelled, "Come quickly, all of you!"

CHAPTER 20

y heart raced. On the horizon, I could just make out the silhouette of a ship headed directly towards us. As it neared, I realised it was white and blue, the colours of police vehicles here in Australia.

"Is that...?" Michael asked, clearly too relieved to finish his sentence. We were all on the deck, looking out to sea, with the exception of Vanessa —I mean, Victoria—who was still safely tied to a chair. "Back inside, all of you," he added. "It's a bad idea to leave her with just one or two people, much less alone."

The storm was over, in more ways than one. It was raining again, but it was relatively light rain. The police must have set sail while the storm was still going and known that it would pass by the time they arrived.

"Is it really the police?" Owen asked. His voice was steady, but the look of wide-eyed hope made me realise that he must have been as scared as the rest of us this entire time.

"Yes, I think so," I said with a smile. "Should someone go and meet them?"

"Why don't you and Mandy go?" Michael suggested. "Owen and I should stay here with Vanessa-Victoria." She was struggling against her restraints so strongly that I thought the chair might tip over. If it did, I didn't want to be around, so I readily agreed, despite the fact I wasn't too thrilled to accompany Mandy. I am sure she felt the same way about me.

By the time we got to the jetty, the boat seemed to be a distance away, and when it finally arrived, it pulled in slowly.

Several uniformed police officers got off the boat, as well as somebody else that I recognised.

"Alder!" I yelled as I sprinted to him. The officers looked somewhat startled at first, but Alder swooped past them towards me, embracing me warmly as soon as he could.

"Amelia," he said, still holding me tightly. "Are you all right?"

It was all I could do to hold back tears. The last few days had been a nightmare, and it was only now that Alder was here that it felt like it was truly over. I hugged him tighter and made a small noise that I hoped he could interpret as 'Yes.'

"I'm glad," he said warmly. We stood in the rain, simply embracing. I wished it could go on forever, despite the uncomfortable looks from the nearby police officers.

When I finally let go of Alder, I noticed that Mandy and all the officers had left.

"Alder, how is it that you're with the police?" I asked, not realising until now that it was more than a little unusual. It was hard to imagine that the police would have let him come along for the ride without some kind of substantial reason.

Alder smiled at me slyly. "I have my ways, Amelia." He winked. "I'll just have to tell you later, when we're alone."

My stomach tightened at the thought of being alone with Alder. I wanted to jump with sheer joy. I let a long sigh of relief. It was all over. "It was Vanessa, who was really Victoria," I told him. "Your article tipped me off."

Alder kept his arm firmly around me, and when we reached the dining room, I saw Owen talking to an older police officer, most likely the man in charge, based on his stance and uniform. Abby and the others were standing behind Owen.

Before I could think to move, a police officer gently touched me on the shoulder. "I'm afraid I'll need you to wait for questioning," he said, indicating the others behind Owen. I nodded wordlessly and smiled again at Alder before I walked away to join them.

"I still can't believe you thought Bazza was responsible," Lisa said sulkily to nobody in particular.

"Oh, come on, Lisa," Abby said with a sigh. "It was a fair assumption. He wasn't supposed to be on the island that night, and he was soaking wet after Sarah had been murdered in the storm. Plus he was found standing over the burning evidence."

"That was just circumstantial evidence," Lisa snapped.

"Hindsight is a wonderful thing," Abby snapped back.

Lisa pouted, but didn't manage a retort. I still felt a bit bad for having been part of locking Bazza up, but it was certainly the right move at the time.

If I could go back in time, obviously I wouldn't have agreed to lock him up, but then I probably never would have come to the island anyway. Perpetually burning food for the rest of my life seemed to be the better option, especially when the alternative involved murder. Then again, even if everything had gone smoothly, no doubt the cooking classes would have resulted in an awful time, anyway.

Before I knew it, I was at the front of the line and the other guests had already boarded the boat. "Name?" the police officer asked me without looking up from his notebook.

"Oh, um, Amelia Spelled," I answered, clearing my throat. I wasn't feeling particularly nervous, but his bluntness had taken me a bit by surprise.

"I just want to ask a few routine questions right now. We'll ask you more back on the mainland, so this won't take too long," he said, scribbling something down as he spoke.

The detective—at least, I assumed he was a detective based on the fact that he was questioning me—only asked quite rudimentary questions. He asked why I had come to the island, to which I had embarrassingly told the truth that my friends had staged a kind of cooking intervention. He responded by being reassuringly unsurprised, before asking me all the other kinds of after-a-murder questions with which I had unfortunately come to be familiar. It was essentially just a retelling of the events of the last few days, with a couple of questions thrown in to test that I was telling the truth.

In the end, the detective seemed satisfied and told me I could join the others on the boat. Alder walked me down to the jetty, his arm still around my shoulders. I think my predicament had given him quite a fright.

When we reached the boat, he hopped in and then stretched out his hand to help me in. I took it with a smile, and tried my best to step up daintily, but slipped on the slick flooring almost immediately. Alder caught me with one arm, the other still holding my hand. He was clearly holding back a laugh, but I appreciated the effort all the same. He helped me back to my feet and the two of us walked inside.

The boat had an enormous undercover area, and for a moment it seemed as though it was somehow bigger on the inside, like the *TARDIS*, only somewhat less exciting, because it was a boat and not a spaceship/time machine hybrid.

The others were sitting around a table, and bizarrely, drinking alcohol. I spotted a bar against one wall.

"I thought this was a police boat," I said with some concern, turning to face Alder.

"It is, right now. They commandeered one. They didn't have a police boat available as they were all needed for emergency services in the storm," Alder explained with a shrug. "It's a lot more comfortable anyway, I'd say."

"But it's even painted with police colours," I said. "Obviously they didn't stop to take the time to paint it."

Alder laughed, and then hesitated. I knew he was making the agonising decision as to whether or not he should tease me with a white lie, but luckily he seemed to give up on the idea. "Just a coincidence, as far as I know. I wasn't exactly part of the decision-making process. I just managed to convince them to let me on board."

Before I could respond, I noticed everyone around me was laughing. Bazza, in particular, was laughing loudly, although he was also staring strangely into the bottom of his glass. They had all gathered at the table, so Alder and I took a seat.

"Oh, Amelia," Michael said with a smile. "Have a drink. We certainly all deserve one."

"Or five," I agreed, taking the cup and drinking deeply. I was instantly filled with regret when I realised I had been handed some kind of intensely strong liquor, but managed to swallow it nonetheless. I would have been mortified if I'd choked and spat it all over Alder, who was frustratingly as dashing and cool as ever.

"Well, Owen and Abby will refund you all for the Beginners' Class, which goes without saying," Michael said with a smile, holding a glass of his own. "However, I'm sure they'd be happy if you all returned for free cooking lessons. I understand that you might not want to go back, given the memories you have recently developed, but that's all the more reason to return. Remember some good times to help override the bad ones," he finished, still smiling, and sat down.

"Even me?" I asked. "They'd let me come back and do the cooking classes?" I was only asking out of curiosity. Nothing would be able to entice me back to that island.

"You should certainly go back," Michael said with a nod.

"And do the cooking classes?"

There was a long, awful silence.

"*You* should come," Lisa said to Alder, breaking the awkward moment in the worst way possible.

"Oh, uh..." Alder stammered.

I cut her off. "I don't think that's a good idea." I knew that the 'cooking class' wasn't quite as advertised, and with both Lisa and Mandy giving Alder a long, hard stare I knew exactly what they were after. "Alder's already an excellent cook," I said sharply, kicking his foot under the table and hoping he got the hint.

Luckily, we were interrupted when the detective from earlier came down the steps. "We're about to cast off," he said, looking over the room. I briefly worried that we weren't allowed to drink the alcohol, but he seemed as though he couldn't have cared less. "Does anybody need anything back on the island, or can we go? The sooner the better, as these storms can come in cycles."

"Um, you did remember to get Vanessa, right?" Michael asked, looking a bit concerned. "I mean, Victoria."

"Yes, of course." The detective nodded. "We're

keeping her detained below deck so that you don't have to suffer through her, well, verbal acrobatics. She's been arrested, and when the forensics team has finished up on the island, we'll have some hard evidence. Combined with all of you as witnesses, of course."

We collectively breathed a sigh of relief. It was good to know that the police had matters well in hand. For the first time in days, I managed to relax. The boat was bathed in a warm, comforting light, and the alcohol kicking in didn't hurt either. The best part was Alder's presence. His arm was now permanently attached to my shoulder, and he was pulling me closer to him. I snuggled up to his jacket, enjoying the comfort and warmth.

The rest of the boat ride was less comfortable. While the rain had stopped, the seas were rough. The boat rocked violently, and the sound of the wind was almost deafening.

At one point, a police officer came to make sure all the valuables were strapped into the boat, and suggested that nobody stand up for a while, which came across as less than encouraging advice. If not for Alder comforting me, I would have almost been afraid for my life. Then again, this was probably the least scary part of the previous few days.

The boat ride lasted about two hours all up, and the last half hour was considerably more pleasant. The rain eased off slowly until it had all but stopped, and a tiny ray of sunshine poked through the thick cloud cover. I noticed it was the first of the sun I had seen since arriving on the island, and it was only at that moment that I realised how much I had missed it.

CHAPTER 21

"Where's the apartment?" Alder asked me as we stood at the entrance to Ruprecht's store, *Glinda's*.

"The apartment is behind the shop. It's just that they share an entrance," I explained. "Just like your apartment." It dawned on me that this was a little strange, but I figured I had become used to the idea.

Ruprecht had invited us over for dinner, supposedly to make up for what had happened on the island. I meant to bring the lightning struck wood, but I'd forgotten it. It was still sitting just inside my front door, all separated nicely into little gift boxes.

Of course, I didn't blame my friends for what

had happened, but it was clear that they felt terrible all the same. Before I could dwell on it, the door swung wide open.

"Ah, Amelia, Alder!" Ruprecht said with a smile. He ushered us in politely and closed the door behind us. Good thing we hadn't been waiting long, too, as it was raining. I had become well and truly sick of rain, but I had to admit that the gloom somehow gave Ruprecht's store a wonderful atmosphere. It was always quite atmospheric, of course, but the rain pelting against the windows gave it an even more otherworldly vibe than usual.

Ruprecht led us through the store, heading directly for his apartment. It was clear that Alder was keenly observing the musty old books and even some antiques. I smiled, thinking I should bring him back here some day soon so he could look around properly. I was happy that my friends had finally accepted Alder after years of wariness, all due to his dark family history.

"Are these for sale?" Alder asked, pointing to a dusty but intriguing Alembic sitting atop a bookshelf alongside several flasks. Ruprecht apparently hadn't heard him, as he was busying himself moving along the maze of antiques.

I turned to Alder and shrugged. "I actually don't know. I always thought he just left those things there for the aesthetic value, but I suppose he might be willing to part with it. Let's come back here soon and so you can have a good look around." Alder smiled and nodded, clearly pleased with the idea.

I looked around the store, which was bathed in soft warm light. A good thing, too, as I certainly did not want to break any of the many antiques scattered about the store. The rain had also caused the musty smell of the old books to intensify, and while it wasn't exactly unpleasant, it was rapidly becoming a little overwhelming.

"Aha!" Ruprecht announced loudly, causing us to jump. "I got it. This silly door has become somewhat of a nuisance in old age," he announced as the door swung open. Ruprecht ushered us through, and the three of us walked to his apartment.

Even before we stepped inside, it was clear that Alder and I were not the first ones to arrive. I could hear talking and laughing as soon as we left the boundaries of the shop itself. I was immediately hit with a wave of warm air, which I very much appreciated. Of course, the rain here in

Bayberry Creek was far more subdued and immeasurably colder than what I had experienced on the island.

Ruprecht led us inside, and it was clear that Alder was somewhat taken aback by the interior. Before he could ask, I decided to put him out of his misery and explain. "Yes, this *is* an apartment," I whispered, realising that it looked exactly like the shop. There were musty tomes and antiques galore, many with price tags. It occurred to me that Ruprecht might occasionally switch stock between his home and shop, but then he enjoyed collecting antiques, so these were probably not for sale. I guessed that the contents of Ruprecht's apartment were worth considerably more than his entire shop.

Ruprecht led us into the dining room, where my friends Mint, Camino, and Thyme were sitting around the large oak table. There were five candles burning in the centre of the table in a pattern of a pentacle, and they were sufficient to illuminate the entire room.

Everyone greeted us warmly, each hugging me in turn.

"I'm so sorry!" Thyme squealed. "I can't believe what happened on the island. I hope you'll forgive us," she pleaded. I noticed that Camino, Mint, and Ruprecht all bore similar expressions.

"Oh, no, it's fine," I said earnestly. "I didn't exactly have a good time, but it's hardly the fault of anyone here. Besides, I'm not sure it was any worse than attending a cooking school that went as planned," I admitted, hoping nobody would notice that I was only half joking.

"Speaking of which, how did you go?" Mint asked. I considered that she was probably just trying to move the subject away from what had happened on the island, but I was all too happy to oblige.

"Well, I only badly injured one person, exploded one utensil, and melted one pan, as well as a couple of smaller things. But no fires!" I announced happily, to which my friends cheered.

"You're improving." Ruprecht beamed proudly as he patted me on the shoulder. I smiled, realising that he was right. It surely wouldn't be long before I could cook something edible. "Let's sit," he said as he motioned me to my chair at the table.

I noticed that the air was thick with the scent of lavender incense, likely intended to help me relax. I appreciated the gesture and breathed it in heavily, enjoying the fragrance. I also noticed that something delicious was cooking, and found myself enjoying the atmosphere immensely. Between the warm room, the soft rain outside, and the smell of lavender and a delicious meal, there wasn't anywhere I would rather have been.

"Oh, Amelia," Camino suddenly blurted out excitedly. "I got you a gift!"

"Oh, no," I said, horrified. I realised what I had said and quickly tried to correct it. "Uh, oh, no, you shouldn't have." I forced a smile.

Camino waved my concerns away and pulled a gigantic piece of purple fabric from a bag before handing it over to me.

"Um, thank you," I said, still wearing the best smile I could manage. I really did appreciate the gesture, but Camino had a habit of getting the worst gifts imaginable. I looked down at what was in my hands and tried to figure out exactly what it was. It was lightly fluffy and had several long bits that I didn't quite understand. It also seemed to have several differently sized holes.

"Try it on!" Camino said excitedly. I felt my stomach sink. It was, of course, a onesie, one of her bizarre, horrible onesies, and she wanted me to try it on right in front of Alder. I briefly wondered if it was possible to get back to the island, but decided just to bite the bullet and get it over with.

"Give me a minute," I said, as I stood up and tried to resist the urge to run away. I walked into the bathroom and held the onesie aloft, finally realising what it was. A gigantic, purple squid suit. It had several strange appendages, and what appeared to be a tiny beak. Did squids have beaks? I thought not. The head was enormous, and nearly as big as I was. I sighed deeply and tried to develop a plan to avoid wearing it without hurting Camino's feelings, but came up blank. I decided I'd just have to try it on.

After what felt like hours, but was probably just a handful of minutes, I managed to get into the onesie—or at least, what Camino described as a onesie, but was clearly some kind of bizarre Halloween costume.

I walked, or rather waddled, back out into the dining room in my new squid suit. Part of me was hoping everybody would just laugh and forget about it, but it seemed as though they all wanted to spare Camino's feelings as much as I did, as they simply stared for a moment, their mouths agape, before simultaneously complimenting me on how good it looked.

I was mortified to be wearing it in front of Alder, though I knew he could appreciate my position and would know that I didn't want to offend Camino. It was hard to admit, but the onesie was also incredibly comfortable, even if I didn't quite understand why somebody would design a comfortable suit with several tentacles and a beak built into it.

"It looks wonderful!" Camino announced happily before drawing me into a tight hug. "I might have to get myself one. I couldn't decide between the squid and the platypus. The bill was so alluring," she said, apparently lost in some bizarre train of thought.

After several attempts, I managed to sit down next to Alder by holding all my tentacles in one of my squid-arms. At least, I think I managed to sit on the chair, but I might have been propped up on the floor. It was hard to tell through the enormous suit.

Ruprecht and Alder were soon in deep discussion about matters philosophical. I heard mention of something called the inverted spectrum problem, and then Ruprecht spoke in an animated fashion about the concept of an entirely physicalist view of the universe. I was happy that Alder and

Ruprecht were getting along so well, but it was the kind of conversation I would have loved to have been further away from. I yawned loudly and rubbed my eyes with a free tentacle.

I snuggled into Alder in my surprisingly warm suit, enjoying the sound of the rain against the windows for the first time in days. The aromas of the house mixed together sweetly, the lavender incense mixed with whatever was cooking—some kind of roast, as far as I could tell—and Mint had just brought hot brewed tea for us all.

It was good to be home.

NEXT BOOK IN THIS SERIES

THE HALLOWEEN SPELL (THE KITCHEN
WITCH, BOOK 6)

The Halloween Spell

This Halloween is maybe Amelia's worst ever. It's one too many tricks and not enough treats . . .

A mysterious woman arrives on Amelia's doorstep claiming Amelia's departed Aunt Angelica did a spell for her every Halloween. She insists that Amelia do this year's spell for her, and that's when the trouble starts.

A murder victim turns up and Alder goes missing. Surely things will be better soon, or is that just witchful thing?

ABOUT MORGANA BEST

USA Today bestselling author Morgana Best survived a childhood of deadly spiders and venomous snakes in the Australian outback.

Morgana Best writes cozy mysteries and enjoys thinking of delightful new ways to murder her victims.

www.morganabest.com

"Ten Thousand Cheering Negro and White Workers Take Over Terminal as Herndon Arrives"
    Daily Worker, Aug. 9, 1934, 2.
"Farrell's Fourth Book Collects Short Stories Written in Last Seven Years" (review of James T. Farrell, *Calico Shoes and Other Stories*)
    Daily Worker, Oct. 8, 1934, 5.
"The Second Macaulay Strike"
    New Masses 13, no. 4 (Oct. 23, 1934): 20–21.
"Stimulating Material on Theatre-Arts Front in Current New Theatre" (review of *New Theatre Magazine*)
    Daily Worker, Nov. 30, 1934, 7.

35   "Exiled Spanish Writers Here to Speak for Literary Groups" (on Rafael Alberti and Maria Teresa Leon)
    Daily Worker, Mar. 18, 1935, 5.
"Poetry" (essay)
    Partisan Review 2, no. 7 (Apr.–May 1935): 32–42.
"Progress or Retrogression" (review of Erskine Caldwell, *Kneel to the Rising Sun and Other Stories*)
    Partisan Review 2, no. 8 (July-Aug. 1935): 61–63.

36   "Poet's First Flight" (review of Muriel Rukeyser, *Theory of Flight*)
    Daily Worker, Jan. 9, 1936, 7.
"Still Ten Years Old" (review of Nathalia Crane, *Swear by the Night*)
    Daily Worker, Mar. 31, 1936, 7.

37   "What Is Happening behind Franco's Lines"
    Volunteer for Liberty 1, no. 15 (Sept. 20, 1937): 1, 4–5.
"A Year of the International Brigades"
    Volunteer for Liberty 1, no. 18 (Oct. 1, 1937): 2–3.
"Franco's Captive: A Catholic Loyalist Was Captured by Italian and German Fascists in Spain. He Escaped to Tell His Story."
    Daily Worker (Sunday Magazine), Oct. 17, 1937, 4.
"Hidden Treasures: The Spanish Loyalists Have Secreted the Priceless Heritage of the Centuries far from the Sight of Fascist Bombers"
    Daily Worker (Sunday Magazine), Nov. 21, 1937, 5.
"Spain's Shirt-Sleeve General" (El Campesino)
    New Masses 25, no. 11 (Dec. 7, 1937): 13–14.

38   "Little Spanish Town"
    Daily Worker (Sunday Magazine), Mar. 6, 1938, 4.

Review of Joseph Wood Krutch, *Edgar Allan Poe.*
    Hillel Review, May 24, 1930.
Review of Victoria Sackville-West, *The Edwardians.*
    Hillel Review, Oct. 10, 1930.
Review of Gorham Munson, *The Dilemna of the Liberated.*
    Hillel Review, Oct. 17, 1930.
"Raids, Redskins—a Gallop for Life and Other Book Notes" (review of Frank Harris, *My Reminiscences as a Cowboy,* and Victoria Sackville-West, *The Edwardians*)
    Daily Cardinal, Oct. 18, 1930, 7, 10.
"'Pure Young Man'—A Winner" (review of Irving Fineman, *This Pure Young Man*)
    Daily Cardinal, Nov. 2, 1930, 7.
"On Recent War Novels" and Review of Conrad Aiken, *John Deth and Other Poems*
    Daily Cardinal, Nov. 9, 1930, 6, 10.

1931   Review of Joseph Van Raalte, *The Vice Squad.*
    New Masses 7, no. 7 (Dec. 1930): 25.

1932   "Jacob Burck—Graphic Historian of the Class Struggle"
    Daily Worker, Jan. 18, 1932, 4.
[Letter to the editor in "The Bear Garden"]
    New York Sun, Jan. 23, 1932.
"A Hunger-and-War Olympics"
    Daily Worker, Feb. 12, 1932, 4.
"Contra la olimpiada de los imperialistas la olimpiada de los obreros"
    Mundo obrero, Mar. 1932, 15, 22.
"The Olympics and Tom Mooney"
    The New Sport and Play: An Illustrated Labor Sports Magazine, May 1932, 4.
"Apoyemos el mitin atletico internacional obrero de Chicago"
    Mundo obrero, June 1932, 10–11.
"Literary Forms" (letter to the editor in "The Bear Garden")
    New York Sun, June 27, 1932.
Review of Whittaker Chambers, *Can You Hear Their Voices?*
    New Masses 8, no. 3 (Sept. 1932): 24.
"Walcott—Former Negro Boxer Sent to Bellevue"
    Young Worker, Sept. 1932, 3.
"Kentucky and the Intellectual." Review of *Harlan Miners Speak.*
    Contempo, 2, no. 4 (July 5, 1932): 3, 5.

1933   "God's Little Acre" (review of Erskine Caldwell, *God's Little Acre*)
       New Masses 8, no. 7 (Feb. 1933): 26.
"For Worker's Children—and Adults" (review of *The New Pioneer*)
       Daily Worker, Feb. 17, 1933, 4.
"Factory Sketches: 'Bertie's' Costume" (sketch, unsigned)
       Daily Worker, Apr. 11, 1933, 4.
"Threaten to Fire Negro Teacher Who Defended Colleague"
       Daily Worker, June 12, 1933, 2.
"Disabled Vet Tells What Roosevelt's 'New Deal' Did for Him"
       Daily Worker, June 27, 1933, 4.
"Farrell's Progress" (review of James T. Farrell, *Gas-House McGinty*)
       New Masses 8, no. 11 (July 1933): 29.
"A Tired Tory" (review of Norman Douglas, *Looking Back: An Autobiographical Excursion*)
       New Masses 8, no. 11 (July 1933): 27.
"A Novel of German Life before Hitler" (review of Hans Falada, *Little Man What Now*)
       Daily Worker, July 8, 1933, 5.
"What Happened at the Daily Worker after the First Six Page Issue Came off the Press"
       Daily Worker, Aug. 15, 1933, 5.
"Red Press" (review of *The Voice of the West End*)
       Daily Worker, Sept. 2, 1933, 7.
"What a World" (on Horace Gregory and revolutionary poetry) (substituting for Mike Gold)
       Daily Worker, Oct. 13, 1933, 5.
"Sergei Radamsky Describes Soviet Music World in Interview"
       Daily Worker, Dec. 28, 1933, 5.

1934   "Farrell's New Novel Portrays Chicago Life" (review of *The Young Manhood of Studs Lonigan.*)
       Daily Worker, Feb. 3, 1934, 7.
"It May Have Been Cold—But Not for Everybody"
       Daily Worker, Feb. 14, 1934, 5.
"East Side Fire Snuffs Out Lives of Eight Workers and Kids"
       Daily Worker, Feb. 20, 1934, 2.
"Upstate Decay" (review of Howard Coxe, *First Love and Last*)
       New Masses, 10, no. 8 (Feb. 20, 1934): 26–27.
"A College Girl Writes about Western Pennsylvania Miners" (review of Lauren Gilfillan, *I Went to College*)
       Daily Worker, Mar. 3, 1934, 7.

"Nationalistic and Jingoistic Speakers in Dem
Hitler Anti-Semitism at Madison Square Garden:
American Legionnaire among Speakers"
       Daily Worker, Mar. 9, 1934, 2.
"Fusion and Real Estate Owners Seek Huge Fed
Profits in Tenement Repairs"
       Daily Worker, Mar. 12, 1934, 3.
"*New Masses* Quarterly Is Real Advance"
       Daily Worker, Apr. 4, 1934, 5.
"Three New Trade Union Papers Make First Appe
       Daily Worker (New York Trade Union Sectio
"Hounded by Georgia Terror, Don West Fights for
Six"
       Daily Worker, June 11, 1934, 1, 2.
"With the Trade Union Papers"
       Daily Worker (New York Trade Union Section
"The LaGuardia-O'Ryan Regime Openly Launche:
Workers of New York City"
       Daily Worker, June 13, 1934, 1, 2.
"With the Trade Union Papers"
       Daily Worker (New York Trade Union Section
"Fight of Sharecroppers in Black Belt against NRA I
       Daily Worker, July 6, 1934, 3.
"Alabama Sharecroppers Fight Onslaughts of NRA
       Daily Worker, July 7, 1934, 3.
"With the Trade Union Papers"
       Daily Worker (New York Trade Union Section)
"Change the World" (on Langston Hughes)
       Daily Worker, July 10, 1934, 5.
"Mayor LaGuardia Reports 'To the People'—Conve
Reign of Terror against Labor—Slurs Over 'Econ
Slashed City Wages"
       Daily Worker, July 12, 1934, 3.
"Reporters Hold Picket Line Solid at Long Island Pr
       Daily Worker, July 13, 1934, 2.
"U.S. Labor History Shows Onward March of Strike
can Workers: Great Railroad Struggles of 1877; Four
in Seattle in 1919; Many Others, Were Prelude to Fri
       Daily Worker, July 17, 1934, 5.
"Seattle General Strike Terror in 1919 Shows How
It—Five Years of Crisis Make Workers Wary of 'Red
       Daily Worker, July 19, 1934, 5.

"Stirring Almaden Defense Draws Enthusiasm of Spain"
  Daily Worker, Aug. 31, 1938, 2.
"Negrin's Slogan, 'Resist to Conquer,' Is Key to Present Loyalist Gains"
  Daily Worker, Sept. 1, 1938, 2.
  Daily Clarion (Toronto), Sept. 6, 1938, 1.
"Behind the Lines—Spain Works to Bolster Defense"
  Daily Worker, Sept. 4, 1938, 3, 4.
"Spain's Metal Workers Hold Key to Victory"
  Daily Worker, Sept. 6, 1938, 2.
"Mussolini's Fifteen Thousand New Troops on Ebro Routed"
  Daily Worker, Sept. 8, 1938, 1, 2.
"Spain Rejoices as Lister Is Honored for His Valiant Record as Leader
in the Republican Army"
  Daily Worker, Sept. 9, 1938, 2.
  Daily Clarion, Sept. 9, 1938, 5.
"Franco Unable to Pierce Ebro Lines"
  Daily Worker, Sept. 10, 1938, 2.
  Daily Clarion, Sept. 14, 1938, 4.
"Vets in Spain Say Dies Witnesses Are 'Cowards, Looters' "
  Daily Worker, Sept. 11, 1938, 3, 6.
"Americans at the Ebro: The Lincoln-Washington Brigade in the Loyal-
ist Drive"
  New Masses 28, no. 12 (Sept. 13, 1938): 19–20.
"Loyalists Tighten Grip on Ebro as Franco Loses Thousands in Most
Desperate Drive of Entire War"
  Daily Worker, Sept. 14, 1938, 2.
"Barcelona Hit by Merciless Air Bombing"
  Daily Worker, Sept. 17, 1938, 1, 5.
"Franco Fails to Dent Ebro Lines in Five Attacks"
  Daily Worker, Sept. 17, 1938, 2.
"Interview with a Captured German Aviator"
  Volunteer for Liberty 2, no. 32 (Sept. 17, 1938): 12.
  Daily Clarion, Oct. 20, 1938, 7.
"Barcelona Cheers New Anti-aircraft; Fascists Routed"
  Daily Worker, Sept. 18, 1938, 6.
"Nazi-Italian Air Attacks on Ebro Fail"
  Daily Worker, Sept. 21, 1938, 2.
  Daily Clarion, Sept. 23, 1938, 2.
"American Negro Surgeon at Spanish Front Appeals for Medical Sup-
plies for Loyalists"
  Daily Worker, Sept. 23, 1938, 7.

"Peasant Is One of Spain's Ace Airmen"
    Daily Worker, Sept. 24, 1938, 7.
    Daily Clarion, Sept. 27, 1938, 5.
"Yanks Fight Firmly in Ebro Defense—Home-coming Nears"
    Daily Worker, Sept. 26, 1938, 3.
"Spain Holds Ebro Firmly; Pleads Arms"
    Daily Worker, Sept. 27, 1938, 2.
"Lardner Is Captured by Fascists in Last Lincoln Boys Fight"
    Daily Worker, Sept. 29, 1938, 3.
    Daily Clarion, Oct. 1, 1938, 5.
"Promotions Reward Lincoln Boys"
    Daily Worker, Oct. 2, 1938, 7.
    Daily Clarion, Oct. 4, 1938, 2.
"Americans and Canadians behind the Lines in Catalonia Join Spaniards
in Honoring Makela"
    Daily Worker, Oct. 3, 1938, 2.
    Daily Clarion, Oct. 5, 1938, 2.
"His Name Was Arnold Reid: An American on the Honor Roll of the
Ebro's Dead"
    New Masses 29, no. 2 (Oct. 4, 1938): 7–8.
"Heroic Chapter for U. S. Boys Closes as Lincoln Vets Pass in Final
Review"
    Daily Worker, Oct. 5, 1938, 1, 4.
    Daily Clarion, Oct. 7, 1938, 5.
"New Franco Drive Echoes Result of Munich Betrayal"
    Daily Worker, Oct. 7, 1938, 1, 5.
    Daily Clarion, Oct. 11, 1938, 2.
"Spain's Communist, Socialist Parties Move toward Unity"
    Daily Worker, Oct. 11, 1938, 2.
"Mac-Paps among Best in Spain Army"
    Daily Clarion, Oct. 12, 1938, 5.
"Spain Renews Its Appeal to World's Workers for Aid"
    Daily Worker, Oct. 12, 1938, 2.
    Daily Clarion, Oct. 14, 1938, 5.
"Poumists on Trial in Spain for Treason"
    Daily Worker, Oct. 13, 1938, 2.
    Daily Clarion, Oct. 14, 1938, 2.
"Loyalists on Offensive Again after Fierce Fascist Ebro Drive"
    Daily Worker, Oct. 15, 1938, 2.
    Daily Clarion, Oct. 18, 1938, 2.
"The Internationals March in Catalonia on the Way Home"
    Daily Worker, Oct. 19, 1938, 2.

"New Documents Show POUM Link with Fascists"
   Daily Worker, Oct. 19, 1938, 1, 4.
   Daily Clarion, Oct. 21, 1938, 3.
"Trial Traces POUM Link to Fascists"
   Daily Worker, Oct. 22, 1938, 2.
"American Sculptor Kept Busy in Spain"
   Daily Worker, Oct. 23, 1938, 9.
"Trotskyites on Trial: Spain's Tribunal of High Treason Hears the Evidence"
   New Masses 29, no. 5 (Oct. 25, 1938): 7–9.
"Spain Says Farewell to Internationals"
   Daily Worker, Oct. 27, 1938, 2.
   Daily Clarion, Oct. 29, 1938, 5.
"All Barcelona Bids Moving Farewell to Foreign Volunteers"
   Daily Worker, Oct. 30, 1938, 3, 9.
   Daily Clarion, Nov. 1, 1938, 2.
"Five Trotskyists Are Sentenced in Barcelona"
   Daily Worker, Nov. 1, 1938, 2.
   Daily Clarion, Nov. 2, 1938, 3.
"Franco Throws Second Line into Stalled Drive"
   Daily Worker, Nov. 2, 1938, 4.
   Daily Clarion, Nov. 4, 1938, 2.
"Bombs Fail to Halt Barcelona Fetes for Lincoln Boys"
   Daily Worker, Nov. 3, 1938, 2.
"Loyalists Score in Air Attacks as Franco's Drive Comes to a Halt"
   Daily Worker, Nov. 4, 1938, 2.
"Loyalists Meet Franco Ebro Attack—Communist Organ Hails Anniversary of Soviet Union"
   Daily Worker, Nov. 7, 1938, 1, 4.
   Daily Clarion, Nov. 10, 1938, 5.
"Ebro Defense Halts Franco Push Despite Big Gun Pounding/Fresh Italian Troops Bolster Fascist Drive"
   Daily Worker, Nov. 8, 1938, 2.
"Surprise Loyalist Thrust Cuts Vital Franco Supply Line"
   Daily Worker, Nov. 9, 1938, 5.
"Loyalists on Segre Push Drive, Take Key Road"
   Daily Worker, Nov. 10, 1938, 1, 2.
   Daily Clarion, Nov. 12, 1938, 2.
"Fascists Lose Heavily in Futile Segre Counter-Drive"
   Daily Worker, Nov. 12, 1938, 1.
   Daily Clarion, Nov. 15, 1938, 2.

"Loyalists Batteries Save U.S. Relief Ship Cargo"
  Daily Worker, Nov. 20, 1938, 3.
"Lister Cites Ebro Drive as Symbol of Loyalist Unity"
  Daily Worker, Nov. 21, 1938, 2.
  Daily Clarion, Nov. 22, 1938, 1, 2.
"Spain Welcomes Gift from Canada"
  Daily Clarion, Nov. 23, 1938, 2.
"Fifty Dead in Savage Italian Air Raids on Barcelona"
  Daily Worker, Nov. 24, 1938, 1, 5.
  Daily Clarion, Nov. 26, 1938, 2.
"German and Italian Arms Flood Spain"
  Daily Clarion, Nov. 24, 1938, 1, 2.
"American, Canadian Spain Volunteers Study, Relax as They Train for
Civilian Life Home"
  Daily Worker, Nov. 25, 1938, 5.
  Daily Clarion, Nov. 28, 1938, 2.
"Many Dead; Planes Bomb Civilians Eleven Times in Day"
  Daily Worker, Nov. 25, 1938, 1, 5.
"Mac-Paps Urge Premier to Aid Repatriation"
  Daily Clarion, Dec. 5, 1938, 1.
"US Boys Leave Spain as Whole Towns Turn Out in Farewell Salute"
  Daily Worker, Dec. 6, 1938, 2.
"Negrin Calls Catalonia to Defense"
  Daily Worker, Dec. 12, 1938, 1, 4.
  Daily Clarion, Dec. 15, 1938, 2.
"280 Canadians are Stranded in Spain by British Officials"
  Daily Worker, Dec. 12, 1938, 2.
"Inspection Shows Loyalist Lines Firm, Morale High on Eve of Push"
  Daily Worker, Dec. 17, 1938, 2.
  Daily Clarion, Dec. 20, 1938, 5.
"Franco's New 'Last Drive': The New Offensive Is Intended to Make
Chamberlain's Job in Rome Easier"
  New Masses 29, no. 13 (Dec. 20, 1938): 3, 5.

1939   "Fair Enough—Architecture of 'World of Tomorrow' Takes Sensational
        Forms"
          New Masses 31, no. 3 (Apr. 11, 1939): 31.
        "The Boys of the Lincoln Batallion"
          Daily Worker, Oct. 1, 1939, 5.
        "The Secret Fighters" ("Edwin Rolfe, author of *The Lincoln Battalion,*
        releases his hitherto unpublished wartime account of the 'guerrilleros'—

those Spanish republican soldiers who fought behind Franco's lines.")
[Part 1 only. Part 2, which is unpublished, is in the Rolfe archive.]
New Masses 33, no. 8 (Nov. 14, 1939): 12–14.

Note on the Bibliography

Rolfe wrote numerous unsigned articles for both the *Daily Worker* and *Volunteer for Liberty* and occasionally wrote unsigned pieces for other publications as well. Since he kept a scrapbook of some of his publications in the 1920s and early 1930s, we have been able to list a few unsigned pieces here. Most, however, remain unidentified. Although the list of his published poems is likely to be complete, the list of his nonfiction prose is thus definitely not complete. Missing pages in the microfilmed copies of the *Daily Worker* make it possible that some signed articles are missing from this bibliography as well.